BAD GAME

A Leveling Up in Love Romance: Book 2

KAT ALEX CRYSTAL

Chapter 1

THE SNOW HAD TAKEN its sadistic time wreaking its havoc on Nick's plans, falling mercilessly all morning and most of the afternoon. Frosty mounds blanketed his small yard, his used Volvo, and the narrow driveway, leaving a shape reminiscent of a woman asleep under an impossibly smooth sheet. A sight Nick was never going to see again at this rate, especially if his car remained trapped in its current icy predicament.

Alabaster hills and valleys obscured the proud landscaping of the suburban street, new worlds brought to life by the storm. In days or weeks, the sun would smite this brash boldness, this hostile, frigid takeover, like a vengeful dungeon master unleashing an overpowered monster on that annoying player in your tabletop gaming party. You know, the one who always ruins everything and tries to keep all the loot.

This was why Nick preferred to run games, rather than be a player. Players got screwed. Players got smothered in a blizzard at the whims of cruel dice and died alone still living in their mom's basement.

He snorted. One obstacle at a time.

Nick shifted his weight in his ratty old snow boots, pondering where to start shoveling. Only the wind's whistling and branches rustling reached his ears, as if he were alone in the world, the only one fool enough to consider this fool's errand. The neighbors' yards remained pristine and smooth, free of signs of human meddling.

They were probably all inside sipping hot chocolate by their fireplaces, if the woodsmoke on the wind was any indication. That did sound like an appealing alternative to squaring off with the storm. The maple tree's ice-covered branches shrugged at him as the wind whipped, as if to say, sorry, kid, but what can you do? Give it up.

But no. Not Nick.

He brandished the shovel and considered again where to start. The neighbors snuggling with their hot chocolates by the fire probably had someone to snuggle *with*. He had a frozen wasteland between him and his someone. Or at least, he hoped she'd be his someone, someday.

Time to roll initiative and get things started.

He chose a spot at random and heaved a mound of snow out of the driveway and into the yard. If he was going to pretend to be good at this adulting thing, he needed to stop losing his gloves. Or letting his mother buy him new ones when he did lose them. With the speed this snow was falling, he would probably lose a finger before he made it into his car.

His phone buzzed in his pocket. He yanked it out and glanced at it. A text from Ashley. *Whatcha doin tonight, stranger?*

Ashley was definitely *not* his someone. Oh, once he'd thought that might be the case. He'd hoped. But they'd been broken up for ages. And while she had taught Nick a few kinky tricks no one would expect a geek like him to know, she'd told him time and again. She wasn't the cuddling type.

At least not with him, he suspected.

She also seemed shockingly incapable of remembering that every Wednesday was game night. Or did she remember and simply not care, hoping to charm him into bailing? Not that that had ever worked.

He also had more fun at game night, much as some might laugh at the idea. Had this been a normal campaign with his friends, maybe he would have been less into it, but this one was special.

His players were not his friends from Campar College or South Peak High School. They were six brave residents of the Truman Stanley Retirement Community. Which incidentally was the part-time workplace of a certain Penny Collins.

He slid the phone back into his pocket and resumed shoveling without answering Ashley, his thoughts drifting to Penny. Was she snuggled up to some lucky bastard, enjoying a hot beverage at the moment? Probably a guy with a nicer car than a Volvo. And an apartment. Did handsome, wealthy beaus cuddle beside fireplaces in suits? Or was there some other James Bond-like outfit for that? Cashmere turtleneck sweater, maybe. Nick glanced down at the flannel he was sporting. Maybe he should change.

She was smarter than him; maybe she'd stay home with this man he could never compete with and not risk the snowstorm.

Maybe he wouldn't even see her tonight.

That slowed his shoveling for a moment. You don't know if she's dating anyone, he reminded himself. This is purely speculation. If you don't investigate the encounter—as in, actually talk to her—you can't know for sure.

Tonight. If she bothered to come out in this mess. And if he succeeded in liberating his car from the snow demons. Tonight he would most certainly talk to her.

But he steeled himself for disappointment. Ashley might be looking for company, but Penny probably had someone to tell her that going to work in a blizzard was a stupid idea. God, what if she had a smart boyfriend, like a neuroscientist or a surgeon or something? Nick would have no chance then.

The dice would likely not roll in his favor this time.

PENNY CAREFULLY SLID the tray of double chocolate raspberry brownies into the oven with both of her pink Hello Kitty oven mitts. She'd hate to put in all that work and drop them on the floor, and Lord knew that was possible. She tried not to think about the mess that had ensued the first time she'd used her apartment's sad little oven. She shut the black enamel door and set the timer.

Her empty, dreary apartment would gradually fill with the heavenly smell, and that would be a start. She'd only moved in a couple months ago and hadn't gotten much more than her kitchen and baking cabinet unpacked. She'd hung her favorite art, though. That had only required a few Velcro strips and hooks. Monet's *Water Lilies* first in the dining room, then Van Gogh's star-filled night by the door, then a more modern and hardly famous scene of a fantasy street in riotous color.

She hadn't hung anything yet in what should have been the guest bedroom, or a spot for a roommate. After Ashley, she'd had enough of that for a while. She hadn't spoken a word of it to anyone yet, but she didn't think there'd be much harm in setting up a studio in there for a little while. Just a little place to paint, away from where the world could see. Away from where her family would see. No harm in that, right?

As long as she didn't tell her mother. Or Cassie. And kept the door shut.

Hanging the paintings was a first step in making the rooms a home, but they didn't stave off the quiet. Silence encroached like a tidal wave, the soft clicking of the stove practically echoing. Or perhaps it was just that there was no one else to hear the faint sounds, no one to worry about disturbing. Maybe she did miss having a roommate just a little.

No, no. Overwhelming silent loneliness was still better than constant pounding heavy metal.

Who was she kidding—it hadn't been the music. It had been the endless parade of guys. Ashley's bed was a freaking revolving door, Toys R Us on Black Friday morning.

And, well, Penny's bed was not. In fact, her store had yet to have its, er, grand-opening celebration just yet.

Hopefully there would not be balloons.

Penny forming a crush on one of those gentleman callers hadn't helped matters one bit. A lot of the guys were a little scary. But not Nick.

She took a deep breath and forced a smile. The silence, the apartment, it was all right. She'd be on her way to work soon, and there would be friendly faces there—Ed, Dorothea, Bob, Betty.

And also Nick.

And double chocolate raspberry brownies to lure them into stopping by her reception desk, if only for a little while.

Her phone buzzed on the counter. Cassie. Sighing, she picked up the phone. "Hello?"

"Penny. Please tell me you are not going out into this storm."

Penny rolled her eyes. "For the millionth time, you're not my mother, Cass."

"Well, Mom is busy with work. Someone's got to look out for you."

"If the storm is so debilitating, I'm sure Mom is trapped at home like everyone else."

"Yeah, right." Cassie snorted. "She's trapped in her office. Working."

Penny giggled. "Well, like she always says, 'Someone's gotta provide for us.' "

" 'Money doesn't grow on trees,' " Cass finished, the lecture familiar to them both. "It's true. Lyle says he's stuck at work too."

Something was off in her older sister's voice. "Everything okay?"

"Oh! Yes, of course. Everything is perfect. Happy as clams over here!"

"Yes, of course," Penny repeated weakly. "But you don't sound happy." If anything, the cheer sounded painfully forced. Sort of like Penny trying to learn to love accounting. If only she could love it half as much as Anka did.

"Oh, Lyle's just been working late a lot. And I'm worried about you. That's all."

"Look, I live a few blocks from work. It's an easy walk. Nothing to worry about." That was a huge reason why she'd taken this boring part-time job, aside from the extra cash. No need to mess with the bus, which would invariably be late or fail to show up on a day like this.

"Didn't you hear about that kid on the news who—" Thankfully, a squeal of laughter cut her sister's story short. "Sweetie, no!"

"How is Lyle Jr.?"

"Oh, a handful as usual," Cassie muttered. A burble of baby talk erupted in Penny's ear as Cass presumably scooped up her one-year-old and brought him closer to the phone.

"Well, listen. I wouldn't want to keep you from his—"

"Not at all. I'm going crazy with boredom over here."

Hence this call, probably. Penny repressed a sigh. Cass had always tried to play the mom in the family, and after she'd gotten hitched and had her little one, she'd kicked the mothering thing into high gear. Big time. Except full-time mothering one child didn't seem to be enough to occupy her.

"I've got good boots, Cass. And remember, money doesn't grow on trees."

"Like mother, like daughter."

"Don't worry about me. I'll be fine."

"Don't forget gloves, and a hat, and—"

"I know, I know. Talk to you later, Cass." Penny hung up. You'd think her sister thought she was still a ten-year-old and not currently finishing her fifth year of college in UDW's accelerated accounting masters program. And of course, listening politely would have just earned her some snowpocalypse horror stories. If there was one thing Penny didn't need, it was to feel *more* nervous.

She swept her colored pencils, pad, and coloring books off her tiny dining room table and into her bag. All right. Enough was enough. Tonight she would talk to Nick. Just one question.

That made her nervous enough.

THE VOLVO *DID* MAKE it out. And Nick had even managed to get his ridiculous amount of gear into the trunk before his mother found him. He was nearly ready to go, the engine running to fight off incoming layers of frost, when he discovered her at the bottom of the basement stairs, arms folded and tapping a finger against the fluffy green bathrobe encasing her upper arm.

Damn. A trap. How was he going to get out of this one?

"Where do you think you're going, young man?"

"God, does no one remember? I run these games every Wednesday, Mom."

"I figured you wouldn't be going in this weather." She gestured vaguely toward the front of the house. "Only nutcases drive in this shit. They even closed the store."

"I shoveled the driveway and the sidewalk too." He grinned, but she only shook her head. Technically, at his age, he didn't need her permission. She hadn't ordered him around for years. But still. Hopefully his olive branch would suffice.

She glared at him. Hmm. That hadn't been a critical failure, but he wasn't out of trouble yet. "Maybe you should get a part-time job as one of those truck operators. I hear the pay is real good."

"One part-time is enough for me right now, Mom."

"We can't live on Bob's kindness forever, you know."

"We won't." He sighed. Not like *she* was taking on more than one part-time job, let alone a full-time one. Whatever. Her business, not his, and he was fairly sure Bob was determined to provide his "kindness" well into old age. "Look. It's fine, I hear it's even going to warm up a bit later," he bluffed. C'mon, c'mon—let the persuasion skill work for me *one* time.

She pursed her lips. "That's not what they said on channel nine. They said it's going to storm its ass off all night."

It wasn't his night.

A rumbling sound cut through his despair, loud even through the basement door. He trotted over and looked out. "See, a plow! And I wouldn't want to let Bob down. I'm sure the whole neighborhood is clear. Don't worry, okay?"

"Nicky, wait—at least take my lucky rabbit's foot with you, or—"

"You already gave me three, Mom. I got 'em. See ya!" He grabbed his keys—latest purple rabbit's foot and all—and darted away.

If you can't beat 'em… you can always run away and hope they don't follow, right? God, he really needed to get his own place.

One problem at a time.

Chapter 2

PENNY'S PHONE buzzed again on the table even as she was pulling on her boots to leave. Thankfully—not Cass this time.

"Hey, Anka." She smiled into the phone.

"Look, I know you need to go, but I just wanted to wish you luck with Sir Dreamy tonight." Anka was smiling too, Penny could hear it in her voice.

"I'm just going to work."

"And Sir Dreamy will be there, right?"

She nodded grudgingly, even though no one was there in her empty apartment to see. "Yes. But I doubt he'll talk to me."

"C'mon. Did you practice any of the pickup lines I left you? You can't ignore a printout."

She snorted. "I saw them. I think I'd have an easier time pretending to be a damsel in distress."

"Does he like that sort of thing? Maybe you should stay away from him then. Guys who want needy girls are usually douches."

"I just meant the whole medieval thing. Corsets. Do you think a corset would get his attention? I have no idea if he wants damsels."

"That's because you never talk to him. And hell yes, a corset sounds brilliant. Who doesn't love a corset? Let's get you one this weekend."

"That's probably not appropriate business attire."

"Who cares? C'mon. You can try a pickup line on me. It'll warm you up to talk to him."

Penny sighed. She had indeed studied them and even high-lighted a few. They lay nearby, abandoned and ridiculous. "No, Ank. I'll never get a word out that way."

"Try one. Guys love getting hit on, they don't care!"

"What if he has a girlfriend?"

"The worst he can say is no." And crush her heart and soul. "Just try one. Just one. Your favorite."

She sighed and picked up the paper. "Can I borrow a kiss? I'll give it right back." Her cheeks burned. Had her apartment gotten excessively warm because of the brownies, or was she just that embarrassed?

"You would pick the tamest one." Anka paused, almost certainly rolling her eyes. "That was pretty good, though."

"I'll never get that out."

"You could just try, 'Hey, Sir Dreamy, how was your day?' or 'How about you Markov chain me to your bed?'"

Penny burst out laughing, fanning herself. She'd thought her face couldn't feel any hotter, but apparently no, it could.

"Just promise me you'll try. Try it on me one time."

"I am not asking him to chain me to his bed!" Much as she might want to.

Anka pretended an exasperated sigh. "This is *such* a missed opportunity. A man with that name, a woman with your under-standing of statistics—"

"No way, Anka."

"Just try the simple version then."

She cleared her throat and glanced at her doorway, the empty living room suddenly cavernous. "Hey, Sir Dreamy, how was your day?"

For a moment, she imagined him walking through the door, running a hand through that tousled brown hair, setting down a bag or a key on a nonexistent table she hadn't set up yet. Stepping closer, gathering her in his arms and telling her—

"Wow, that sounded almost natural," Ank's voice cut in, snapping her out of her daydream. "You sounded excited, interested even. You can do this. So you promise you'll try?"

Penny sighed again. "Okay. I'll try. I promise."

"Good luck, Pen. Go for it. You deserve it. What's the worst that could happen?"

Trudging through the snow down the street, her brownies clenched in both hands and her satchel of art supplies over her shoulder, Penny pondered exactly that. What was the worst that could happen? He could tell her he'd had a shitty day and storm off. He could laugh at her and not even answer. She could mess up midword—as she was wont to do—and not even get the sentence out. She could say hey, look into those dreamy brown eyes, and forget what she had planned to say. Even something as simple as "how was your day" had failed in the past. And then she would die of awkwardness.

But maybe that was better than dying an old maid. Or maybe not.

"Hey, Nick, how was your day?" she practiced. "How was your *day*? How *was* your day? *How* was your day!"

A man popped out from behind a tree, a snow shovel in his hands, and gave her a funny look. She snapped her mouth shut and hurried past. No need to die of awkwardness before she even arrived.

Still, she muttered it under her breath a few more times for good measure.

She stomped the snow off her boots on the porch to the activities center of the Truman Stanley Retirement Community, swung her way in, and headed for the desk. Festive shamrocks danced across the walls and the front of the reception desk, even though Valentine's Day was barely over. Lena jumped up, as though she'd been waiting to sprint away, and headed straight for the coat closet.

"Oh, thank God you're here. I was so afraid you wouldn't make it through the snow."

"I can walk." Penny dropped her bag by the door, eager to get the treats set down before she somehow tripped and spilled them everywhere.

"Really? I've gotta keep my shifts before yours all winter." She grinned at Penny and jogged toward the door.

Penny had just begun settling down at her desk when a tall, lanky form in an orange coat came up the front sidewalk, carrying a heap of boxes and bags. Tousled short brown hair peeked out from under his hood, but his face was in shadow. Her pulse quickened.

Lena greeted him as she opened the door. "Oh, hey, Nick!"

"Hey, Lena," his heavenly voice called.

"How was your day?" Lena tossed off casually.

Fuck. That was *her* line. What was she going to say now?

She turned to watch their casual conversation, practically vibrating with a mixture of jealous rage and elation. He shrugged. "Could have been better." He glanced at Penny as pushed his hood back with his free hand and smiled. Fucking water in the desert, that smile. His short beard made it all the better, and eyes not far from the color of her brownies twinkled. He pointed at the rec room. Then he seemed to glance anywhere but at her for a moment.

She sighed and nodded. He wanted to set down his things before signing in. He usually made several trips. He headed back out after Lena, who waited for him to return before leaving. She'd been in a hurry before. And now she stopped to chat with him? Lord knew she called him a dork half the time and acted like he was an awkward social project who needed to get out and exercise more, maybe play some football, and not the most brilliant, adorable, handsome man she had ever—

"Do I smell brownies?"

Bob's voice cut through her thoughts. "Yes. Want one?"

"Did you make them for us?"

She nodded. Bob was leaning on the reception desk and clutching his notebook and pencil to his pale blue dress shirt. He'd record the details of whatever game they all played in that notebook.

"You're such a sweetheart. Hey, you should play with us tonight. I bet Nick could handle another player just fine."

"Oh I think he'd like to handle her all right," grumbled Ed as he shuffled past. Penny rolled her eyes. Ed was always saying things like that. Classic dirty-old-man shtick, although he was sweet as a caramel underneath.

"I'm supposed to be working, Bob, but that's nice of you to offer." She smiled at him.

He waved her off. "Nobody's coming to visit on a night like tonight. Amazing you two made it here! You both must have been pretty determined to get here." He gave her a wink that she couldn't decipher.

She shrugged. "I walk over, so it's no big deal."

"Oh, that's right. I keep forgetting. Eighty'll do that to ya. Still, come play with us!"

"It looks… complicated."

He frowned at her. "Aren't you studying to be an accountant? If you can handle that, this is nothing."

Of course, Nick chose just that moment to come back through the door. To her surprise, he stopped, as if he were listening for her answer, rather than continuing on to set down the second load of boxes tucked under his arms.

"Uh… yes" was all she could manage.

Bob snorted. "Well, then it should be easy for you. I always failed at math, and I'm making due. Right, Nick?"

"Right, what?" he asked.

"I was telling Penny she should play with us. She brought brownies." Bob raised an eyebrow as he pointed at her pink-towel-covered tray.

Nick's eyes widened. Oh, God. He definitely did not want her to join them, no matter what Bob said. That was a "deer in the head-lights" look if she'd ever seen one.

"Oh, I don't need to trouble you," she said quickly. "I'm sure you have too many players already. And I'm working. I should be attending the desk—"

"Nonsense," Bob muttered under her words. "Nobody's coming in tonight except you two crazies."

The door rang its bell behind Nick. Realizing he was blocking the doorway, Nick hastily stepped out of the way. Penny's stomach clenched as her eyes caught on her art bag, forgotten on the floor by the entry.

Right next to Nick's feet.

Nick tripped, then caught himself. But one box slipped out, and dozens of tiny pieces scattered across the floor.

"Oh my gosh, I'm so sorry!" Horrified, she rushed around the desk to help with the mess.

Bob started to bend down, then stopped. "Nick, uh, why don't you give me those boxes and I'll, uh… go over there." Bob grabbed them before Nick could even respond and hustled away. Penny frowned. What was that all about?

She fell to her hands and knees and started gathering up the items, which looked like small toy soldiers but in animal and fantasy forms like bears, wolves, orcs, elves, knights, and goblins.

Oh, Sir Dreamy, you even carry knights around with you. She sighed inwardly. Tiny ones, but still.

He crouched down too, a moment later, and she was surprised to realize he was barely a foot away from her.

"Really sorry, Nick——" she started.

"Oh, that's not your fault. I should have had it shut better. Maybe a rubber band. My fault."

"No, no, I shouldn't have left my bag there. You could have wiped out——"

"Really, its fine." He sounded sincere, reassuring even. She looked up to find herself already pinned by those glorious brown eyes gazing down from above. She could see flecks of gold in them at this distance. He was… oh Lord, he was smiling at her. "I didn't know you want to be an accountant."

Fear jolted through her as she forced some words out, trying to qualify that somehow. "Well, uh— I don't exactly— 'Want' might not be the right word."

He tilted his head and frowned, pausing in picking up the little men.

"I'm just good at math, need something stable," she muttered. "What are these?" She held up a particularly fascinating one, hoping to change the subject away from her. And her lack of sincere interest in her chosen profession.

"Oh." He sounded disappointed. God, was he an accountant? Had she insulted her brethren somehow? What had she even said? How had she known him for this long and not figured out his job yet? "These are miniatures. Game pieces, basically."

"This one is especially beautiful. Look at the detail around the belt, must be six different colors there. That must have taken a skilled hand. Or are these done by a machine?"

He blinked.

"Sorry." She flushed and hurried to scoop more up. Nobody cared about painting like she did. Oh, they might pretend, but their eyes glassed over faster than a puddle at the North Pole.

"No, no. I was just…" He blinked again. "I painted that one."

"What? *Really?*" His eyes widened at her enthusiasm. Shit. Too much, Penny, too much. "I didn't know you painted," she added, trying to sound more casual.

"Oh, I don't. Well, just miniatures."

"Oh." Her hopes dimmed. It would have been so nice if Sir Dreamy liked to paint as much as she did. But of course, life didn't work that way. He couldn't be so handsome and seem so kind and actually like things that she did. She should be rejoicing they were even *speaking*.

"I mean, I wish I did," he said. The words came out in a rush. "But I seem to suck at everything except miniatures. They give you structure, you know? And I can imagine what a real person or creature would look like. Don't have to get the shapes right. You can focus on color and shadow."

She snuck in another furtive glance and tore her eyes away when she realized he was more focused on her than their task. He looked… actually interested in the conversation.

She was suddenly very aware of the square of his shoulders, the way he loomed over her, casting a shadow, the woodsy, spicy scent of him. Was that… patchouli?

"Oh, yes. Coloring books do the same thing. Less stress." They had almost gotten all the miniatures; only a few stragglers remained.

"I have some bigger dragons you might like. Why, do you—"

"Nick! Penny! Happy Wednesday!" boomed Dorothea's singsong voice.

"Hello, Dorothea," Penny replied cheerily.

"Hey!" Bob snapped with surprising urgency. "I, uh, come see this, Dorothea, will ya?" Penny frowned. Bob was acting… strangely.

Dorothea swept past them with one more wave, her sapphire-blue tunic and thick gold necklaces garish but also adorably her. Penny had to admire that voice; Dorothea was not a woman who would freeze up, fail to find the words she was looking for.

Nick looked from Bob back to her. He opened his mouth, closed it, then opened it again. Neither of them moved to pick up the last handful of remaining figurines.

"He's right. You're, uh, welcome to play with us. If you want."

That wasn't exactly a rousing invitation. She frowned. He probably just felt pressured into it. But she didn't want to turn him down. Perhaps if she didn't respond now she could figure out later how to handle this. Text Anka for input. Although her outgoing friend would probably just tell her to use pickup line number forty-two on him or something. It *had* worked on Ahmed, Ank's boyfriend. Maybe Penny should take her pickup-line study more seriously.

Penny looked down at her lap, searching for how to dodge a response, then reached for the nearest figure.

Her hand bumped into cool, smooth skin. Him. They'd been reaching for the same one.

Both froze. She glanced up and met those brown eyes again, daring herself not to look away as a jolt of electricity shot through her.

"You know, we could—" he started.

"Aw, Nick and Pen, look at you two." Betty strode up the main hallway. Her hair was curled and her jumpsuit purple velour today. She and Dorothea were decked out.

Penny snatched her hand away, mortified. Nick couldn't want that. They weren't together. Guys didn't like such implications when they weren't warranted. Even from sweet old ladies.

"Ah, come on, Betty, stop interrupting," Bob snapped.

Penny blinked. Interrupting what? She jerked up and dove for the few figures that had spilled the farthest away. When she turned, Nick had also risen. She held out the figures to drop them in the box. Instead, he held his hand out and took them, time slowing as his fingers brushed her palm.

She barely concealed her shiver.

He put the figures in the box in slow motion, his eyes still trained on her. He hesitated, then turned away.

Ah. Over so soon. Disappointment threatened to overwhelm her. They'd talked longer than ever, but it was mostly all because of him. And her stupid bag.

The night would go on, and she'd watch him from afar, laughing with the group. He might stop by for a brownie, or he might not. He might say goodbye on the way out the door.

But mostly, it was over.

How was she going to go another week without another chance to talk to him? He'd been interrupted how many times—what had he been going to ask her?

Hell, *no*, it couldn't be over yet.

"Uh, Nick?" she blurted. Shit, what now?

He stopped quickly and turned. "Yes?"

"How—uh, how was your day?" she croaked, her voice catching a little and stumbling through the words. Oh Lord, could that have gone any more awkwardly?

The smile he gave her nearly stopped her heart. Such smiles were worth risking death by awkwardness. Her stomach flip-flopped as she stared into those brown eyes. "Much better, now."

A tingle flew through her. "Oh, uh, glad to hear it." Oh, great response. Think—what next, what next? She hadn't even tried to plan for this, she'd been so sure she'd fail the first step. Damn it.

"Yours?"

"My what?"

"How was your day?" His smile broadened. Probably in direct proportion to the redness of her face. God, his beard was so cute though.

"Oh, ah, boring. But I made brownies. Do you want one?" Wow, she was on a reckless bender here. This could only end badly.

He hesitated. Yes, this was going to be bad. Definitely bad.

"They're double chocolate raspberry—"

"I forgot to have dinner," he said at the same time.

She stared, unsure how to interpret that. Was that a yes or a no?

"Did you have dinner?" he asked.

"Uh, no. I usually eat after work. I guess it would make sense to eat dinner before dessert." Her shoulders slumped. Duh. Who wants brownies at dinnertime?

He shrugged, a sudden twinkle in his eye. "Depends on the dessert. Some desserts are so good, it's hard to wait."

Was she having hot flashes? Was the retirement center on fire? Was that an innuendo or was she just that desperate? "Uh, where do brownies fall on that spectrum?"

"I'm not sure. It depends on the brownies. Would your day be… less boring if we ate together?"

Her eyebrows shot up. "What?" she choked out.

"Do you want to have dinner when you're done with work and *then* try the brownies?" His slow voice felt heavy with meaning. Was he… flirting with her?

She stared, too stunned to respond.

"Unless you assure me that I absolutely shouldn't wait." His smile broadened to a grin, all the way up to his cute crinkled eyes.

Answer, Penny. Answer, damn it! Get voice systems back online!

"Sure. Uh—I mean, I'd love to have dinner, not that the brownies can't wait. They're just brownies, they're not a big deal."

He frowned. "I heard they were double chocolate raspberry. And you worked hard on them."

He'd even been listening. Was she going to faint? "Well… yes.

Dark chocolate. No nuts. Do you like nuts? And they *are* warm now." Just like she was.

He took a step closer and eyed the tray. "Nuts only interfere with brownies, if you ask me."

The perfect man. He was the perfect man!

"But I should go set up. Dorothea's trying to get Betty to abandon her character and play a barbarian. That should be interesting. Feel free to come and play, Penny. If you want. No pressure." He smiled again and walked toward the rec room.

Come and play, Penny. Those eyes. That voice. Fuck. She was lucky she had few actual duties other than watching the sign-in sheet and answering the phone. It wasn't like she was going to be concentrating on anything.

Other than him.

She dragged her art bag behind the desk and sank into her chair. Then she fumbled in the pocket of her puffy purple coat, searching for her phone.

Suddenly, Nick's face popped up in front of the reception desk. She gasped, clutching a hand to her chest.

"Sorry." He grinned. "Forgot to sign in." She nodded and pretended to be very interested in her phone while she watched him out of the corner of her eye. He scribbled something and threw down the pen. "You close at nine, right? I'll meet you here then."

She stared again, then stuttered a quick, "Yes, yes, I'll be here. Are you sure you'll be done by then? I know sometimes you guys are still playing when I leave. I can wait if—"

"Don't worry, I got this," he said, still grinning, and strode off.

Well, holy shit. How did he know what time her shift ended? Did she have a *date*?

When she was sure the game had started up, she texted Anka. *Okay don't freak out but I think I just might maybe almost sort of have a date.*

What?!?!?!! came the frantic response. *Omg can you go home on a break and shave your legs?*

Penny snorted. *Are you out of your mind? In this weather? Besides it's just dinner after work. That is so not happening*

Don't be so sure. Did he flirt with you? Does this mean you used your pickup line?! Omgz!

He kind of did, she texted back. *I think he did? We are in an old folk's home, remember? They'd probably have heart attacks if I said half the things on that pickup line list.*

Whatever, Anka texted back with a silly face.

We mostly talked because I was the cause of massive chaos and made him drop half his stuff. But I DID ask him how his day was!

Wow! You're getting some tonight for sure.

It's just dinner!

I was kidding. But you know, you might if you want to. ;)

Did she want to? She glanced over at Sir Dreamy. He rolled a die, and they all leaned forward to see what had come up. Maybe she'd see how dinner went.

Oh, who the hell was she kidding?

Her grand-opening sign was up, and she was ready for Sir Dreamy to come charging in any minute now. Maybe there should be a ribbon-cutting ceremony. Er, no, that sounded kinky. She squirmed in her seat. Well, maybe kinky wouldn't be so bad. What if he *was*, er… into creativity in the bedroom? What if—

She was really counting chickens without any eggs to hatch. She cut off the errant thoughts and focused on the short term.

Dinner.

NICK HUMMED to himself as he packed up his figures, his pencils, his gridded sheet. So much stuff, but everything he lugged here added another dimension to the experience. Every time he packed up his car, he vowed to take a little less next time, whatever he didn't use. But when the next week rolled around, chances were he'd bring more than ever.

The dice clinked as he threw them in his bag: shimmering blue, gold swirled with red, solid forest green. He checked his phone. Eight forty-five. Perfect. Enough time to load his car up and be on time for Penny.

He glanced over at her for the thousandth time that night. He kept thinking—or was it hoping?—that he felt her watching, but she never seemed to be. Her blue eyes were usually trained on her phone or her desk, busily working away on something that he doubted was work for the center. A curtain of long, straight blond hair hid exactly what she was doing most of the time. Her crisp white button-up and soft gray corduroys were the same as she usually wore, a uniform of sorts. Nothing out of the ordinary for her, even if it was sharp enough to be interview attire for most girls he knew.

Was he reading too much into this? Dinner after work wasn't much of a date. She could easily be thinking of it as between friends, casual acquaintances. Which was pretty much all they were.

And while he'd tried to look presentable because he'd be seeing Penny, he'd also shoveled snow for hours before leaving and wasn't exactly looking his best. Should he have tried for another night?

But waiting sounded awful.

He'd never gotten many words out of himself in her presence, and tonight, it had been so easy. What if it never happened again? What if next week they went back to polite pleasantries and silence? What if neither of them broke through again? He'd had to act while he could, imperfect situation or not.

He reached for his keys he'd left… hmm, where had he left them? He could have sworn they were here on the table. He could have sworn he'd seen them only a minute ago. But… they were nowhere on the table.

They were nowhere anywhere.

"Thanks for coming out in the snow tonight," Bob said, approaching.

"No ice cream?" Nick replied. His players had promptly headed off to the "late night" ice cream event for those who could stay awake for it, all aflutter when he'd said he couldn't join them because he was having dinner with Penny. Hadn't Bob gone with them?

"Oh, I'm headed over, but it looked like something was wrong. Everything okay?"

Nick frowned, folding his arms across his chest. "Well, no. I can't find my darn keys."

"Well, do you need them to eat dinner? You weren't going to drive anywhere."

Nick shrugged. "I guess not. I hadn't figured that out yet."

"Penny lives nearby. She'll know where to go. Why don't you go catch up with her and I'll look for your keys? You have a Volvo, right?"

Hmm. If he stopped now, he could be early to their almost-date. He wasn't typically an early kind of guy, except for dates. Not annoyingly early. Just enough to show it was important to him. He craned his neck, trying to see if Penny was at her desk, if she was ready to leave or still working.

She wasn't there.

"Go on, go. I'll pack up. Doc probably thinks I should have less ice cream anyway." Bob winked at him and started opening one of the boxes Nick had already packed up, presumably to search for the keys.

"Thanks, Uncle Bob. Look for a red dragon claw keychain, and at least one purple rabbit's foot." He grabbed his coat. So much for Mom's dismembered animal foot bringing him luck. "You want to call me when you find them?"

Bob nodded. "Go on, kid. Knock her dead." His eyes glittered with amusement.

Nick narrowed his eyes. "What do you mean?"

"You know exactly what I mean. You two are always mooning over each other. I'd tell you to take her dancing, but I hear they don't do that anymore." Bob grinned.

Not in the polite and social sense that Bob remembered it, no. Would Penny ever want to go dancing? He couldn't imagine her coming out of a club, dressed like it was eighty degrees even in a snowstorm, stumbling down the sidewalks in extremely hot, extremely impractical shoes. Penny wore smart shoes. Shoes he couldn't help but thinking of as sexy, but… he couldn't imagine her in spiked stiletto platforms. Nothing like Ashley used to wear.

And that was exactly what he liked about her.

So Bob had him figured out. "Wait—us two? I mean, I've noticed her recently, but…"

"Recently?" Bob gave him the side-eye. "I'd say it's been at least three months."

Nick swallowed. They had been playing for four. Nick didn't really want to admit it, since he'd finally broken things off with Ashley only three months ago, but the truth was that he had "noticed" Penny pretty much right away. He hadn't been sure if these members of the Greatest Generation would like the game, but one look at her, and he'd been determined to make it work. At least for one more week. One more chance to walk past her again, smile at her while he signed in, struggle to think of something to say.

"All right, maybe it's been a bit longer than that," he admitted. "But wait—you noticed something about her too?"

Bob grinned. "She's not so quiet around everyone else."

He blinked. "She's not?"

"Nope. And she watches you when she thinks no one's looking. Trust me, Nick. I may be headed to a walker one day or another, but I know women. I've loved a few, for a lot longer than you have, and that one likes what she sees. Now promise me you'll be a gentleman."

"I'd never be anything but, Uncle Bob." He smiled as he shook Bob's outstretched hand. He and Bob didn't necessarily have the same definition of what a gentleman was, but Nick could certainly promise to live up to his own standard.

He was going to do his absolute best not to screw this up.

Chapter 3

WHEN PENNY RETURNED from the restroom, having made her best effort with the lip gloss she'd been lucky to find in her purse, Nick's lean form was leaning against the reception desk.

His back was to her as he waved to someone heading out. Most of the visitors were leaving the retirement community activity center for the night. He had his jacket on already, one of those puffy down ones in a fluorescent orange. Had he been waiting long? Hell. She took one more deep, steadying breath, then headed into the desk area for her bag.

He turned. "Hey! Guess what, I can't find my keys anywhere. Uncle Bob offered to look for them for me."

She tilted her head. "Bob is your uncle?"

"Sort of. I can explain over dinner. But is there… somewhere good we can walk to? Probably better than driving in this madness anyway. Maybe the plows will have gone through by the time we're done?"

She sincerely hoped they hadn't. She hoped they ran out of salt and the roads were impassible even for plows and Bob never found his keys. Ever!

Wow. The wave of ill wishes was not her typical style. So… she really hoped he was stuck here? With her? Was this really her plan? Did she have it in her to lure him to her apartment somehow?

Insanity. Talking to him had been nigh on impossible three hours ago. Dinner was enough. Her apartment was a ridiculous dream. Why not wish for winning the lottery while she was at it? Maybe they wouldn't even make it through dinner before he found somewhere else to be.

And yet, if opportunity came knocking... who was she to turn it away?

She hurried to answer his question. "Yeah, there's plenty of places nearby. Are you going to come back here then? When he finds the keys?" If he finds them. Perhaps someone had stolen Nick's car. Hmm, that one seemed like she was going a bit far. And there would be police reports he'd have to file, keeping him from her apartment.

Nick nodded. He was smiling still, even up to his eyes. He seemed genuinely happy to see her.

"Okay, well, I'll leave this bastard here then," she said, pushing the bag under the desk.

He snorted. "Is it heavy? I can carry it if you want."

"Oh, no, it's fine. I don't need it." She grabbed her coat from the hook on the wall behind her. She tucked her phone and wallet into her pocket and rounded the desk area. "But yes, it is heavy."

"Well, I would usually try to pick a place, but do you have anywhere in mind?" He started forward as she reached him, clearly with some goal in mind. Ah, the door. He opened it with a grand flourish and a mock bow, and she let out a slight giggle as she marched past him out into the snow.

"Usually, huh?" What exactly did that mean? Like, when he usually set up a date? Oh, God, how was she ever going to figure out if this was a date or not? He said nothing in reply, thrusting his hands into his coat pockets as he caught up to her side. She tapped her chin with a gloved hand. "Hmm, let me think."

Dates. Dates. What to eat on dates. She hadn't gone on a ton of them, but food that caused awkward bodily interactions was probably not ideal. Indian might not be the best choice, although that was one of her favorites. There were decent burgers at the diner, but it was also heavy fare. Hmm, Wednesday night meant Vi was doing Tarot at Eden. Was that a good thing or a bad thing? Eden was also a lot darker than a diner, and quieter, and… more intimate. More like where you'd go on a date. A shiver ran down her back.

Was she really up for suggesting a place where half the seats were only pillows?

She glanced at him beside her, at the sharp, intelligent glint in his eyes, the fine profile he cut against the frosty parking lot. Oh, yes. Yes, she was. "Well, there's Jake's Diner. Or Eden is pretty good, if you like veggie and vegan food. I have a friend doing Tarot readings there tonight."

"Wow, really? That's fine with me. I eat everything."

"Okay, it's just down here. Do you want to get your cards read? I'm sure she'll read ours for free if you want."

He glanced at her sharply at the word "ours," something unreadable in his gaze. Was that overreaching? Was she freaking him out? Probably. But the expression had almost seemed like… hope. "What's the worst that could happen?" he said, smiling. "Sure."

She tore her eyes away from him. She should be watching the sidewalk anyway to make sure she didn't face-plant and imprint herself as a graceless klutz in his mind forever after.

They walked in silence for a moment. A dark-colored SUV passed at a snail's pace, still throwing slush at the sidewalk. Seeing its approach, he reached out, took her shoulder, and guided her to the inside of the street, switching places with her. Luckily, he dodged the incoming slush in the process. His hand lingered on her shoulder for a second, throwing a rush of delight through her. Was he going to leave it there? But a moment later, his hand retreated back into his pocket.

Oh, Sir Dreamy. You're even sort of chivalrous. Perhaps a lot chivalrous, because hey, the night was young. She swallowed. She tried to think of herself as an independent woman, and she didn't particularly like the implication that because he was a man, he *ought* to get slush splattered on him, or the idea that somehow having a vagina meant that she deserved not to get slushed. Ideally, neither of them would be pelted with dirty snow. But… given that he had taken the initiative, it was terribly sweet. If this lasted beyond tonight, if they ever went on a second or third or fourth date—or dare she dream more than that—she'd show him he didn't have to sacrifice or suffer for her. Couldn't they be equal in all things? Even in suffering, even in inconveniently being pelted with snow?

But hardly anyone cared enough to notice snow splashing in her direction, let alone actively protect her from it. Her mother and Cass had always cared when it suited them, more than when Penny really needed it. She didn't look at him, afraid her gaze would reveal too much.

"What's in the bag?" he asked instead.

"Bag?"

"Your bag you left at the retirement center."

"Oh." She blushed. "Art supplies. It's just that it's rather boring work, and I don't really have many people to deal with most days, and…" She trailed off, struggling to think of a justification.

"Cool. What kind of art do you do? I'm assuming the painting stays at home, or are there acrylics in there?" He smiled, his brown eyes bright and warm.

She blinked. He… knew what acrylics were? He'd remembered what she'd said about painting? He asked you a question, she reminded herself. He's waiting for an answer, not for you to stare into his eyes dreamily. "Uhhh. C-colored pencils," she stammered. "Not my favorite. Most of my favorites… don't travel well. Messy. Impractical." Like the entire hobby, and the intensity of her love for it. Highly impractical.

"What are your favorites?"

She shrugged, trying not to reveal the joyful chaos under her surface at these questions. Instead she answered obediently, soberly, a little afraid he might discover her silliness. Smart girls didn't spend their time on these things. Surely, he wanted a smart girl, didn't he? Some guys didn't, but surely Nick would. Ashley was sure brilliant. "Pastels. Charcoal. I really love tactile tools. Ones you can rub and shape with your hands, feel the roughness of the paper," she said, trying to sound nonchalant and failing. "Feels more alive."

She glanced at him, trying to gauge his reaction. The light of a streetlamp silhouetted him for a moment, jaw tense, a movement in the muscles of his neck. Did he just swallow?

Why was she focusing on such insignificant details?

He cleared his throat. "Do you have a favorite choice of subjects?" She tilted her head at him. That wasn't the kind of question Mom or Cass would ever ask. That was the question of another artist. The pounding of her heart, which had just eased, surged again. Could it be? Was it possible he could have as impractical a love as she did stashed away in his heart?

"Oh, any old thing," she lied. "Although... I do like flowers." No, that sounded silly. Something smarter. "And dragons."

They quieted while they carefully crossed the street. While most of the sidewalks had been dutifully attended to by nearby owners in the last few hours, the road was in worse shape. Only a few cars had left any tracks. In fact, there were probably more footprints in the snow than tire tracks.

"Just a little farther," she said. "That red door right up there."

Again, he jogged ahead a few steps and opened the door.

"Penny!" Tamira called even as heat rushed out of the restaurant and Penny scampered inside. "And—who is *this*?"

Penny blushed. She opened her mouth, but nothing came out.

"I'm Nick." He held out a hand and shook Tamira's firmly.

"Nice to see you out, Penny. Nice to meet you, Nick. No takeout tonight?"

Nick raised an eyebrow. Penny blushed even harder, something she hadn't thought possible. "Not tonight, thanks. A table for two, please."

"Sure." Tamira studied her screen, its white light casting her lovely dark features into relief. Her purple lipstick was an amazing shade. Penny wished she had half the boldness with color on her face as she did on the paper. Or half Tamira's boldness would do too, perhaps.

"Is Vi reading tonight?"

"Oh, she couldn't make it through the snow. Although I think she just doesn't want to leave Jack on a night like tonight."

Penny smiled. "Probably not. New boyfriend," she said in explanation.

His eyes widened, clearly not understanding. What did he *think* she'd meant?

"Vi has a new boyfriend—Jack. Not much incentive to go out, I guess. Not that I would know."

"I'll be right back. Let me check one thing." There was a glint in Tamira's eye. Oh, Lord, this could be bad. Perhaps she shouldn't have gone somewhere she knew people.

"We both apparently had some incentive to go out," he said as Tamira vanished. He glanced back at her with that meaningful look in his eyes.

"Well, I had to work," she said, regretting it almost immediately.

"Oh, of course." His eyes twinkled. "And I absolutely could not have let Uncle Bob down. They're dying to get back to town and level up."

Silence stretched between them for a moment, his gaze fixed on her, hers darting around to look just about anywhere else.

The inner door chimed as Tamira reappeared. "Follow me, you two."

Penny did not like the sound of that. She trudged after Tamira, regretting every choice of the night. Tam led them to a very dark corner floor booth, the kind with only crimson pillows on the floor as seats, a black lacquer backboard, and a low table with golden inlay. None of the tables nearby were seated. Much of the restaurant was empty in fact, probably because of the snow.

"Will this work?" Tam asked.

Penny hesitated, not having any idea if this was a huge mistake in Nick's book.

"Looks great," said Nick, and he went around Tamira to the far side of the booth, leaving the closest seat for her.

She sank down onto the pillow with relief.

Tamira smiled. "Can I get you something to drink?"

"Green tea, please," Penny said. Something warm to take off the chill of the storm.

Tamira gave her a funny look but wiped it away quickly.

"What?" Was that not something you should order on a date? What about an after-work dinner with someone you hardly knew and had no idea where you stood with?

"I'll have the same," Nick said quickly, and Tamira scooted away toward the kitchen.

Penny wanted to melt against him, fairly certain he had only ordered tea because she had and not because he would ever do it on his own. She did get so bold as to scoot her pillow two inches closer to him.

She had to figure out if this was a romantic thing, pronto, before she drove herself crazy. She busied herself with taking off her coat and purse instead. Did her usual white button-up say date as well as work? Maybe she should unbutton it a little…

"It was the darnedest thing, I swear my keys were right there." Nick was totally at ease. If he had seemed slightly nervous earlier, those signs had vanished now.

"Maybe Bob will find them. You said he's your 'sort of' uncle?"

He smiled sheepishly as he picked up the menu. "Sort of. He's not related to me. He was actually my mom's landlord for a while, and we all got to know each other. Kind of… filled a gap, I guess. Games at the—oh my God, lemon ricotta pancakes."

She laughed. Maybe she hadn't offered such a bad choice after all. "The strawberry French toast is good too."

"Maybe I should get some actual dinner. Like a grown-up or something." He glanced at her.

"I'll probably get a chickpea burger. Or maybe a hummus wrap. Those don't really count for dinner, that's more of a lunch thing, isn't it? Maybe I should order a salad." That was what girls were supposed to order on dates, right? Something that wasn't the size of their face.

"No, no, you should get whatever you want." He frowned at the menu.

"Chickpea burger it is."

"Oooh, wait. Grilled 'cheese.' This is hard. So are you vegan… all the time? Does that make any sense?"

She smiled, but he kept glaring at the menu. "No. I didn't even eat anything vegan until I met Tamira."

"How did you meet?"

Luckily he missed her slight blush. "We're in a fortune-telling club together."

He glanced up. "Really? Oh, like the tarot reader?"

"Vi's actually a PhD candidate. The fortune-telling is just for fun."

"Ah. So do you read tarot too then?"

She shook her head, glad he was asking the questions. He'd run out eventually, and then it'd all be her. Or silence. Most likely silence. "Just a little. I dabble in some more… esoteric types. The Asian *I Ching*, for example. I'm just learning from the others for now. It's a fun excuse to get together." Also nice to get together with other smart and whimsical ladies who liked much less serious things than drawing dragons in their spare time.

He smiled. "Kind of like D&D."

"I guess? You're not just learning about that, though. You seem to know an awful lot about it." She'd never had any friends that played. Well, until now. If she could count older folks she worked with and a guy she'd barely spoken to as friends.

He shrugged. "There is always more to learn, Penny-san."

A giggle escaped her, but she had nothing to follow it with. Silence threatened.

"I give in. Grilled cheese and tomato soup it is. Like Bob used to make. Except I don't think anything he's ever cooked could be served here."

She grinned at him, unsure of why that made her so happy. She wondered just how much Bob meant to him, but before she could figure out how to ask, Tamira swung by, took their order, and dropped off the teapot, pouring them each a cup. Penny cradled the small, round earthenware in her hands, alternately blowing on the tea and letting the steam warm her face.

Belatedly, she realized she should be saying something. "So, what do you do, Nick?" Please don't say accounting, please don't say accounting.

"I'm a photographer. Graduated last May."

She stilled, glad her enjoyment of the steam hid her surprise. So he *was* an artist of a sort. This was too good to be true. The fact should delight her, but now it was starting to freak her out. This was too lucky. There was no way it would actually work. "What kind of photography do you do?"

"I'm still trying to find my place. I did a bunch of weddings last summer and liked it, so I might focus on that."

"Weddings, really? What's that like?"

"Nerve-racking. But fun. I did a mix of my own gigs and helping out with a few more established friends as a second camera."

"Second camera?"

"You know, taking pictures of the groomsmen horsing around while the lead photographer is with the bride?"

"Oh. Cool. No, I haven't been around many weddings." Or any.

"No one in your family?"

"I have a small family. Just my mom, my sister, and me, really."

"Ah." A frantic silence—at least for her—settled for a moment. They both took hasty sips. "Me too."

What did she say to that? Panic rose as the silence lengthened. Ask him about something—anything—that will keep him talking for a while this time. "How did you get into photography?"

"Oh, uh…" He looked down, and Penny sensed this was not the topic she was looking for. "When my parents got divorced, I had this therapist who suggested it. A way to reclaim some control, assert my view of the world." He shifted uncomfortably but then seemed to relax a little. "It did do the trick. It's nice. Relieves stress. At least, when I do it for fun. Weddings are not relaxing." He grinned, propping up a knee and draping his arm over it as he leaned back. "I do some retouching for friends too. I might try to get into fine art or stock at some point. Just trying to figure out what will pay the bills."

"Yeah." She nodded knowingly. "That's why I let my mom and sister talk me into accounting."

"Why?"

"Well, I can't make money with art."

He shrugged. "Sure you can. Why not?"

She stared at him, mouth hanging open. His eyes darted to her lips and back up again. Oh. She probably looked like an idiot. "No one's ever asked me that before. People always just assume…"

"Have you tried?" He smiled, taking the sting out of the words.

"Uh… well, no."

"Well, I mean it isn't easy. But how do you know if you haven't tried?"

She shrugged. He had a point. A scary one. What if she should have tried? What if she was making a huge mistake with the accounting degree? Of course it couldn't hurt to have something to fall back on… But what if it was all a huge waste of time?

Worse, if what he said were true, if she actually wanted to try… Mom would flip her shit. And Cass would probably show up at her apartment and refuse to leave until she'd talked some sense into her little sister.

"I do like math," she muttered.

"There's a fair share of math in photography too." Had he leaned closer while she was staring at her tea, or was that wishful thinking?

She sat quietly for a moment, rocking the nearly empty teacup. "I don't even know how you would do that."

"Do what?"

"Make money with art."

"I only know about photography. Unfortunately, you can't paint weddings. Although some people do portraits at them, don't they?" He raised his eyebrows hopefully.

She shook her head in an emphatic no. Only if they wanted portraits that turned them into fairies and princesses and knights. And took hours.

"But my friend is a freelancer. Does commissions. I could send you her email."

"Really?" She grabbed his upper arm in excitement, and his eyes locked on her grip. She snatched her hand back, not having meant to invade his space. "Sorry. I mean, that would be… amazing. Yes, please!"

He stared back without reacting for a second too long, and she had no idea what she'd said to cause that, but eventually he nodded. He pulled his phone out of his pocket. "Give me your email?" He handed it to her, notepad open. "Or, er, I can text you if you want."

She typed both her email and phone into the note, making absolutely certain to make no errors. She checked them a third time before handing the phone back. Did that qualify as him getting her digits? No, no, he was just doing her a favor. A professional one, at that.

He cleared his throat as he put the phone back in his pocket, but he was smiling wider now, and when he settled, he was even closer. Their shoulders were nearly brushing. "Shoot, where did we leave the brownies? I still need to have some after this."

"I left them on the desk."

"Bob may have eaten them all then. Maybe that was why he was skipping the late-night ice cream social."

Penny snorted. "I can make you some more if he does."

"Really?"

"Yeah, they're easy."

"Promise?"

She quirked an eyebrow at him. "Promise. But I wish I had half the social lives they do."

"Well, that would leave you less time for baking brownies. And spontaneous vegan dinners."

"True, true." She smiled. "Did you have a hard time getting over here?"

He shook his head. "The highways were pretty clear. Just my driveway was a lot of work. I thought I might miss the whole thing. Every time I got half of it clear, it felt like the other side filled back in."

"Something I don't miss about having a car. Not that walking or taking the bus in the snow is much better."

"Getting anywhere in the snow is always a pain, whatever your mode of transportation. Although I suppose I haven't tried dogsled."

"It's nicer to stay in. Cozy."

His warm brown eyes met hers with a surprising intensity. "Yeah, it is. And yet we're both here."

She snorted, glancing around at the restaurant that looked emptier by the minute. "One of the few, the proud, the brave."

The desperate?

He opened his mouth to answer, but before he could, he frowned and reached for his pocket. "It's Bob," he said. "Speak of the devil. Maybe he found my keys."

She stared out the front restaurant window as he and Bob talked, trying to give them privacy. The snow continued to fall heavily, dancing white under the glow of the streetlights, contrasting with the cozy darkness of the restaurant.

"Are you serious? Crap." He glanced at her, covering the mic for a second. "He says he can't find them." He went back and listened again. "Not anywhere? Did you look under that couch? Maybe someone kicked them."

She took a deep breath. That snow was falling something serious. He'd have a hell of a time digging his car out a second time, and now later at night the roads might not be clear any longer. She tried not to think too hard and elbowed him softly.

"One sec, Bob. Yeah?" He covered the mic again.

"That's really falling hard, Nick."

He squinted out at the snow. "Damn."

"Unless you brought a shovel with you, you may have trouble getting out even if he does find your keys."

Nick frowned, then started to turn back to Bob.

"You could… stay with me if you like!" She winced as the words came out awkwardly loud.

Nick froze, and his eyes locked with hers, now even more intense than before. Heat raced through her. He didn't say anything for a long moment. Maybe he was weirded out that she'd offered. Maybe he just wanted to be friends.

"I have a futon," she added to see if that put him at ease.

Did his face fall? He turned back to Bob and the phone, and she averted her eyes back to the window. "Were they under the couch?" He sighed. "Ah, well. Hey, Penny says she has a futon I could stay on. Probably safer than driving anyway, right? And then you can get to the ice cream social." There was a pause. "What? You already went? You sure looked for those keys hard. You what? Damn it, Uncle Bob." Nick shook his head. "All right. Oh, they are? All right. I'll stop by in the morning, and hopefully I can find them then. Good night."

She turned back to him, but he was still fiddling with the phone, jamming in a text to someone. For a moment she thought she saw Ashley's name fly past in his texts, and a small jolt of fear went through her. Did they still talk? Maybe he still liked her. Maybe he was still *with* her. No, no, Nick wasn't the kind of guy to ask a girl on a date if he had a girlfriend. But then, with Ashley's revolving-door policy, maybe there was more nuance or flexibility to the situation than Penny understood.

What was she getting herself into?

If anything?

She knew he'd dated Ashley. On and off for a while. Mostly she'd seen pictures on Facebook, and she'd spotted him at their apartment occasionally back in the day. But he hadn't noticed her then. Or even seen her.

But she'd noticed him. He'd always seemed like the one that least belonged with Ash. The one Penny was most jealous of, frankly. The one of Ash's conquests that Penny most wished she could steal away and protect from the inevitable hurt that Ashley inflicted on pretty much everyone around her. Lord knew it had taken Penny long enough to recognize that, and even longer to extricate herself from it.

How long had it taken him?

She wasn't going to bring up Ashley, though. Not tonight. Not with the insane way this night was going. In fact, she banished thoughts of her former roommate from her mind.

"Sorry." He jammed his phone back into his pocket without explanation. Not that he owed her one. "So Bob says they're locking up early, cause of all the snow. So no bingo until eleven tonight, and we are being separated from our brownies. Oh, shit, and your bag. Is that okay? We could run back there now."

She waved it off. "It's just pencils. I can get it tomorrow. And make more brownies too."

"That sounds like a decadent breakfast."

She grinned. "Or you could stick around for lunch?"

His eyes widened, and she realized she might have implied more than she intended with that phrasing. She ducked her head. Of course, she'd love for him to stick around for dinner and the rest of the week and month and maybe never leave. At least it wasn't inaccurate. But she was probably way past freaking him out now.

Their food came, thankfully saving them for a moment. The burger was heavenly, and she devoured half of it before even coming up for air.

Huh. That silence hadn't been so awkward. Or had she just not noticed it?

"We could watch a movie, if you want," she said between stuffing fries in her face. No, she wasn't nervous eating. Not at all. "It's still pretty early."

"Sure."

"I just moved in, so my place is still kind of a mess. Have my TV and futon set up, though."

He nodded. "Do you like the place?"

"Quieter than my last place!" She grinned, mostly to herself this time. "But yeah, it seems nice so far. And I have the top-floor apartment, so nobody stomping around above me while I'm trying to do homework." Or pounding the headboard against my wall while I'm trying to sleep.

He smiled. "That must be nice. When do you graduate?"

"Next year. It's an accelerated five-year program."

"Fancy."

She shrugged. "Not really. But if I take my certifications after I graduate, I'll be able to do a number on your taxes."

He glanced at her and smiled crookedly. "You don't seem like a typical accountant. Will you have a pink calculator?"

She narrowed her eyes and stuck out her tongue before she could think better of it. "My calculator is sky blue, thank you very much."

He laughed. A nice sound, warm and sincere.

"It might have a pink bow. And a face I put on with stickers."

"Maybe you should work for the IRS, then. You're going to scare the shit out of people."

She shook her head. "Probably 'cause they won't think I'll be able to do their taxes with a calculator like that."

"Well, can you? I'm sure you can. So you can laugh in their faces."

"We use computers for these things most of the time, Nick."

He grinned and took another bite of his sandwich. "You sure it's okay I crash with you?"

She nodded, not meeting his eyes. "Not like you have anywhere else to go at this point."

"Still, it's very considerate of you. I guess maybe I shouldn't have gone out in this weather after all."

Penny shrugged again. "Oh, I don't know. It seems like it's working out all right to me." She dared a glance up and found him staring at her. Those eyes were going to bore into her soul, at this rate. She looked back down and took another huge bite of her burger so she had an excuse not to say anything further.

He laughed softly. "I think you may be right."

Chapter 4

NICK COULD HARDLY BELIEVE he was following Penny to her apartment. Sometimes the dice hate you, but sometimes you get lucky. Dare he hope literally? Well, it remained to be seen if either of them were getting lucky tonight. Try as he might, he hadn't been able to swing the dinner solidly into date territory, and he was still not sure if this whole futon thing was simply her being hospitable.

Fortunately, he had at least a two-hour movie to figure it out.

That afternoon, he hadn't even known if she had some neurosurgeon boyfriend waiting to beat him up for glancing at her. And wishing he was curled up with her by a fire. Oh, and fantasizing about her too. Now, at least, it appeared she didn't have a boyfriend.

He hoped.

They were quiet for the short walk back, and although he had more to ask her, he was nervous too. Maybe he should have taken another shower after shoveling all that snow. Maybe he should have shaved better. Maybe he should have tried harder to get any details about boyfriends present and past who he might be compared against. Even if Bob was right, and Penny did have an interest in him, it couldn't be as strong as his was. He'd never liked a girl so much, for so long, without even talking to her. This had to be some kind of record for long-delayed courtships.

The elevator up to the ninth floor was a quick ride, and she opened her door to apartment 914. Slate-gray carpet, cardboard boxes, and bare white walls were everywhere—she wasn't kidding when she said she hadn't unpacked much. But a Monet and a Van Gogh caught his eye, as well as a bustling fantasy city above the futon.

"Wow, that's nice," he said, approaching to take a closer look. "Good size too."

"Thanks. Um, I'm going to use the restroom. Be right back."

"Okay."

He pulled out his phone and checked to see if Mom had responded. *A friend's house? Whose?* came the first text. *You better be being safe, Nicholas Jacob Markov!* said another. *If you're dead, I'll kill you!*

He shook his head. *I am fine, Mom.*

An answer came back right away. *You didn't say who the friend was.*

God, a girl, Mom, okay?

Oh. OH. That's the big deal with going out in the storm. Why didn't you just tell me you had a date?

He shook his head again. *Good night, Mom.*

Be safe, Nick. Good night.

He glanced at his other texts. Ashley had sent him three more, all inane versions of the same thing, trying to get his attention. Would responding and telling her to fuck off be better or would that simply encourage her? He wouldn't reply. It was over. It was over three months ago. He had nothing say to her.

He checked the battery. Thirty percent. He better switch it off, since he didn't have a charger. He powered it down and put it back in his pocket.

He glanced around. A pink, fluffy Hello Kitty blanket lay over the back of the blue futon, along with puffy square pillows in the shape of a cupcake, a piece of sushi, a penguin, and a panda bear, all with bright and cheery grinning faces. So Penny.

Sushi. Yes. That's where he should take her next time. If there was a next time. There had to be a next time.

He should probably sink down onto the couch with the panda and penguin, but he couldn't help himself. He wandered to the window to check out the snowy view, then spotted a small desk light on in the next room. A large desk was littered with a computer and dozens of scattered drawing implements and paper. One drawing was partially sketched out, but a stack of finished ones rested on the corner. The top one depicted a dragon in shocking shades of tangerine and eggplant.

He flicked on the overhead light to get a better look.

WHEN PENNY CAME out of the bathroom, he wasn't anywhere in sight. Shit. Light shone from the second bedroom. She procrastinated the inevitable discovery that he pitied her poor attempts at art by hauling the extra pillow and blanket off her bed for the futon. What else could she do? If she delayed long enough, would he wander back out and not say anything? Damn her for having left the place mostly clean. Time to face the music.

Creeping up slowly, she found him leaning over the desk, leafing through a stack of pastel and ink drawings. As she leaned against the doorway, gripped with horror that he was looking at the random pile of horrendous sketches she'd left out the day before, he glanced up.

"These are *fantastic*. Are these yours?" He dropped his gaze back to them, studying them intently.

"Uh... yeah."

He stilled at the tone of her voice. "Oh. I shouldn't have come in here. You might not have wanted to share. Sorry."

She waved it off. "No, no. It's fine. I've hardly unpacked anything else."

"You should really post some of these online. People would love them." He held up one she particularly loved, a purple-and-black dragon in front of an orange sunset. "Damn, Penny."

She flushed now. "They're just a few studies, nothing major."

"Well, I need to see what you consider major then."

She blushed harder. "I, uh, it's all packed up still," she lied.

He set the drawings down and turned toward her. "Movie time?"

She sighed with relief. "Sure!" He followed her back out to the living room. "So I have a huge library of anime, Netflix, *Firefly*, or— I know—*Lord of the Rings*?"

"Heh. If we really get snowed in here, we might need all that. But any one of those sounds great." He flopped down on the futon. He was sitting on her futon. Lord in heaven!

"Which one is your favorite?"

"Assuming you've watched them all?"

"Of course."

"Maybe *Two Towers*? Is that weird to start in the middle? I like seeing Saruman go down."

"The Ents are my favorite. Two it is."

She slipped the disk into her player and flopped down right next to him. In addition to the pillow and blanket she'd brought, her futon was crowded with pillows, which thankfully gave her the excuse to sit close. Not touching, but close.

Normally she would curl up on the couch, or get comfortable somehow, but all those movements would take her farther away from him, so she sat awkwardly still and wooden. Like a mannequin. Like a scarecrow propped out on the porch for Halloween.

She tried to focus on the movie with moderate success. She'd watched them more than a few times, looping when the apartment was too quiet, when the loneliness was too much—or when Ashley's visitors got too loud. He had never been particularly loud, though.

Her eyes darted toward the bedroom wistfully, but she bit her lip and tore her gaze away. Remembering nights—and days—when she'd known he was there in her apartment, so close and yet so far away, when she'd longed for him in spite of it all… Despair settled over her. God, what was she thinking? How could anyone who'd fucked someone as gorgeous and experienced as Ashley for years ever want a virgin accountant? No, a virgin accounting *student* too shy to even say hello most of the time. What a silly, stupid dream. Just like the paintings. All of it—a nice hobby, a nice dream. Embarrassingly foolish.

She needed to just come down to earth and get a grip on reality. Sir Dreamy was a fun hobby, but he was never going to be interested in anything other than sleeping on the couch.

She abandoned her wooden posture and squirmed around, trying to find a way to get her feet under her without moving too far away. She could enjoy his shoulder next to hers for the duration of the movie. Despair or no despair, she wasn't going to be able to stop wanting him. She'd just stop hoping so hard.

Before she'd found a comfortable position, though, his shoulder moved too, the heat leaving her arm as he reached up to scratch the back of his head. Ugh, she was probably weirding him out. If she were kind and hospitable, she'd move those pillows so he could get the fuck away from her.

As she settled down and forced her attention to the screen and its soaring soundtrack, a warm weight settled across her shoulders, tugging on her hair. She reached up absentmindedly to swish it out of the way, to the side, away from him, exposing her neck in his direction, and her fingers brushed soft flannel and then warm skin.

Her heart might pound out of her ribcage. His arm. Her shoulders. Lord in heaven, he'd put his arm around her. It really *was* a date! She hadn't been crazy, hopeless, *or* embarrassingly pathetic! Well, maybe she was some of those things, but not for making eyes at Ashley's ex.

Sir Dreamy was actually interested in her.

Or at least interested in putting his arm around her while they watched *Lord of the Rings* on her futon.

She shifted a little again, and his hand tightened on her shoulder, shifting her in the process an inch or two closer to him. Against him now. She stared at the TV, fighting hyperventilation and trying to memorize this moment, this feeling, this everything. Engrave it on her soul forever. A scene or two passed, the air around them tense. Then she felt his eyes on her. How long had his gaze been trained in her direction instead of the movie? She reveled in it for a moment, but gradually realized he wanted her to look at him. To return his gaze.

Why?

Did she care? She took another moment to build up the nerve and then turned toward him. Those clever, laughing brown eyes with their golden flecks locked with hers, and she stared, rapt, captured by the sparkle in them, their intensity boring into her. Like they saw into her soul. She was frozen still, a rabbit before a lion, and she longed to turn back to the movie, if only so she could prevent confessing all her truths to the demands of that stare.

She glanced down at her lap, away, only for a second of relief. But she couldn't bring herself to look back. Or move. Fuck. What was going on?

SHE DROPPED HER GAZE DOWN, and he immediately missed the expression in her blue eyes, intense and beautiful and not something he understood for certain. Her shoulder radiated warmth through her shirt to his hand, and she'd swept her blond hair to the other side, the curve of her neck teasing him, close enough to reach out and taste...

He could barely believe he'd pulled it off. Getting his arm around her could have been much more awkward, but it'd gone off without a hitch. She had only moved slightly closer, really, but she hadn't objected or put him in his place when he leaned in. And now she'd lifted her face toward his, met his gaze, and surely she must know he wanted to kiss her. This all was a good sign, right? That she hadn't invited him up here purely out of a sense of duty and friendly hospitality?

Time to find out.

He bent closer, leaning in and pausing just an inch from her lips. Her breath came in hot quick puffs against his skin. A soft rose flush played across her nose and cheeks, and her lips were shiny pink like a strawberry Starburst.

He waited. He wanted to be sure. She had to want it too. That was perhaps the most important part of being a gentleman that he could think of, so he wasn't going to mess this up.

She didn't move.

Another moment passed. Fuck. Fuck fuck fuck. A sudden fear

dawned on him. Maybe she *was* trying to be nice, inviting him up here. And he was that creepy dude, reading too much into it, wasn't he? She was super freaked out now and didn't know how to respond. Maybe she'd hoped he'd cut it out after the arm-around-her thing. He'd thought… at dinner… and with the arm maybe… But no. Still, she sat motionless, her eyes downcast at his lap.

She was probably scared shitless. She was probably regretting having ever agreed to go to dinner with him. She'd even brought out the pillow and blanket beside him. That said it clearly. You're sleeping on the couch. Idiot. Fuck fuck fuck, why hadn't he figured that out sooner?

He jumped to his feet and strode to the door, regret flooding him. "I should go," he said quickly, his voice rough. God, he wanted her more than he'd realized.

But if there was anything he didn't want to do to Penny, it was make her feel pressured. Or that he might do something she didn't want. Or that he would abuse her generosity by trying to take advantage of her. Fuck fuck fuck.

He wasn't "that guy." He would put her first, damn it. Even if Penny wasn't interested in him yet, maybe he could convince her someday. But he couldn't if she thought he was a fucking asshole. Good going, jackass. Way to ruin your chances before you even got started. And she didn't even know anything about his past yet.

He grabbed his coat, tucking it under his arm for speed. He shouldered his bag, then reached for the doorknob. He couldn't look back at her. He'd figure out how to straighten this out later, apologize, something. He pulled the knob but nothing happened. Oh, yeah, the deadbolt.

He had no idea where he was going. Maybe he could walk home in the snow. Maybe he could google how to break into his own car. And hot-wire it. Maybe he could get someone to open the door at the center and crash on that couch in the rec room. Would Bob vouch for him? Would he still be awake if Nick called him? He could look for his keys again at least. He turned the deadbolt.

A squeak came from behind him, so quiet he almost didn't notice. He froze, the knob turned in his hand.

She cleared her throat. But when she did speak, her voice was barely a whisper.

"Don't go."

Eyes wide, he turned. He released the knob, but his hand remained poised in the air just above it. Had he heard that right? She was standing, her form lovely in the dramatic light, one side lit by the small lamp, the other by the goddamned *Lord of the Rings*. God, she was perfect. She hadn't moved from beside the futon yet. Was she... shaking? "Penny, I'm sorry, I didn't mean to—"

She took a step sideways around her coffee table. She faltered for a moment, then walked the whole way over to him. His body responded as she drew closer, so many thoughts of so many nights and mornings so much closer to real. And yet she was more than any of the things he'd imagined her, just looking at him right here.

She reached out and laid a hand on his forearm. He stared at it, helplessly fixated on the heat from her fingers through the flannel shirt. "There's nothing to be sorry for."

"Yes, there is, Penny, I'm—" He reached for the doorknob again.

She put her other hand flat on the door, as if she might hold it shut if he tried to open it.

Interesting.

His eyes locked with hers. Did the intensity in hers match his? Was there really an electric current flowing between them through her hand on his arm? Or was he just some horny asshole putting her in an awkward position?

He put his hand on the knob.

"Please," she murmured.

He tried to conceal the shiver that shot through him, shutting his eyes at the intensity of it. That voice. That word. A wild fantasy of her on her knees, soft cotton-candy lips parted, her hands reaching for him, flashed through his mind. He shook his head, trying to shake it off. Get it together, Nick. That was about the most ungentlemanly thought he could imagine at the current moment.

"It's much too snowy to go anywhere," she whispered.

Oh. The words cut through his fantasy, but heat still pounded through him. Was that it? Was she only worried for him? But he released the knob in defeat. There was nowhere to go. The center was locked up, and the buses weren't coming. Maybe she didn't want to kiss him, but maybe he could salvage this awkward situation another way rather than just running away.

He spoke as he his coat and bag back down in defeat. "You're very generous to be concerned about me. And to offer to let me stay here. If you're tired, we can go to sleep. On the couch. I mean, I can go to sleep on the couch. Alone. I really appreciate…" What could he possibly say to salvage this? "You're a good friend." There. That should put them firmly in platonic territory where she wanted them. Right? He was babbling.

She frowned. Why? Fuck fuck fuck, he had screwed up again, but this time he wasn't even sure how.

"I'm never in bed before midnight. Movie's still good. We can finish watching if you want. Or we can retire if you prefer," she said with a swallow he didn't know how to interpret. "How about something to drink? Tea? Wine?"

"Wine would be great," he said, then immediately regretted it. He'd dug himself enough of a hole already. The last thing he needed to do was get drunk.

"Red or white?"

"Red."

She floated into her kitchen, his eyes following her body hungrily as she moved before he could stop himself. Shit, more creepy behavior. Get it together, man.

"Oh darn, I only have blush. Rosé? I'm not sure. I don't know anything about wine. It's pink."

He snorted. That figured. "Whatever is fine. I like it all."

Yes, getting drunk would be a bad idea. And yet, when she placed a tumbler of wine in his hand, he took a long swig. Something had to get him over the mortification of what had just happened.

Chapter 5

WHILE NICK SANK BACK onto her couch, momentarily placated, Penny fled to the bathroom—and her phone. Frantically she texted Anka. *He tried to kiss me, then before he did, he stopped and tried to leave! Wtf does it mean!*

She eyed herself in the bathroom mirror while waiting for Anka to reply. It was late, she might be busy. Or asleep.

Wait? What? Who? Where are you? came the reply.

Nick! I mean, Sir Dreamy! In the bathroom.

Whose bathroom?

Oh. My bathroom. I invited him to stay over. We had dinner! He's on the couch. There's much too much snow out there. As if that explained how this had all happened.

Holy crap! Go you!

But he almost just ran away after trying to kiss me! What the hell, what do I do!

She banged her head against the door for a moment, then took a deep breath. He might hear that. She straightened herself in the mirror. Should she put on more lip gloss? Less? Lipstick? If she came back out in red lipstick, would the message be loud and clear? Not that she owned any, but hypothetically.

Hmm. Did you try to kiss him back? Or did you do that deer in the head-lights thing you do?

Funny, she had used that phrase in her head to describe Nick earlier in the night. That seemed a long time ago. *Oh, I froze up big time. You know me. Statue girl.*

Maybe he thought you invited him up for you-know-what, and when you didn't kiss him, he thought maybe you didn't.

Huh?

Maybe it occurred to him at the last second that you just invited him up there as a friend. Nick's words by the door came flooding back to her. Alone. Friends. Couch. *I mean, you have to admit if you thought he was butt ugly and didn't actually massively want him to bone you, you might be a little freaked.*

Oh, fuck.

I mean, good on him for not wanting to be that dude.

What do I do. It'd been too long. She left the bathroom and headed for the kitchen to open one of the three bottles of wine she had above the refrigerator. The nice one, for sure.

Lay one on him, came Anka's reply. The phone vibrated loudly against the quartz countertop as she was pouring the first glass. She stifled a groan. How was she going to do that?

She peeked out the kitchen pass-through. He was also focused on his phone, one hand rubbing his forehead, looking distressed. She had no idea how she'd "lay one on him" in that position.

How do I do that?

She grabbed the tumbler and walked into the other room to hand him the glass. He took it gratefully, with a nice smile and thank-you, but distress still creased his features.

From the kitchen, her phone vibrated three more times.

He raised his eyebrows as she blushed. "Everything all right?"

"Oh, yeah, that's nothing," she muttered, dying to look casual as she practically scampered back to her phone.

Jump in his lap and go for it! came the first text. Then, *Or get more drunk first. Are you even drinking?* And finally, *Or put your hand on his knee. Even you might be able to handle that one.*

Hmm. She might indeed be able to handle that one. It wasn't

exactly Pickup Line Thirteen levels of boldness. *We did just break out some wine*, she replied.

It'd been awkwardly long. What if he thought she was calling the cops or something insane?

Gotta go. She mashed her fingers into the phone until it was in silent mode and then threw it in the corner. She grabbed her glass, took a huge swig, and poured some more.

What was the plan? What was she going to do?

She stood for a moment or two, feeling short on time, and came up with nothing. Perhaps she could just sit down beside him again, and maybe he'd try again and she could just lean toward him this time. And if he didn't, she could plan her next move out there, not while she was in here doing who knew what.

It was a terrible plan, but it was all she had.

She strode out, trying to walk in some kind of sexy fashion, although she had no idea if she was pulling that off, and then plopped back beside him on her coach.

His arm felt missing behind her neck. It had felt so natural to have it there, and it would feel so right for him to simply put it back there now. But he didn't.

The movie had marched on, over their drama. She could ask him which parts she'd missed if she wanted to make conversation, but… No. She'd seen it too many times, anyway. She sat in silence, barely aware elves and dwarves and hobbits struggling on-screen, much more acutely aware of his body beside hers.

Could she do it? Could she just move her hand over a few inches and rest it on his leg? Like it was no big deal?

She tried. Her hand twitched. Fuck. She tried again. And failed. What if Anka's interpretation was wrong? What if he had realized something but had nowhere to go? What if her breath was terrible? What if he didn't want her? Climbing in his lap might get super awkward then.

This was never going to work. She couldn't even get her hand to move. She was going to die an old maid. She wanted to groan but stopped herself. What if… what if she could try to explain what had just happened? Maybe in some sort of roundabout, casual terms.

"Hey, Nick?" She took another long gulp of wine. God, what if he got annoyed with her talking over the movie? But it was too late to turn back now. "You ever get… nervous?"

"Of course. All the time." He looked down at her, frowning and completely uninterested in the movie too.

"What do you do when you get nervous?"

"Uh, I have a tendency to get jumpy. Fight or flight and all that."

"Is that what just happened," she muttered, not really a question. He raised an eyebrow, but she waved off the comment and trained her eyes on the TV. "I tend to… freeze up. Especially if it's about something I really care a lot about."

He stilled. "Deer-in-the-headlights style?"

She snorted. "Why does everybody keep using that phrase today? It's kind of… morbid. Isn't the deer about to get hit by a car?"

"Things you really care a lot about, huh?" He sat forward, as if he was trying to get her to look at him.

She winced. "Yeah." Had she revealed more with that statement than she'd intended? She hid her embarrassment behind another hasty gulp from the wine. Or three. What would he think if he knew she'd had a crush on him for over three years? Maybe longer. She tried not to think about it.

To her surprise, he set the tumbler down on the coffee table and slid to his knees on the carpet in front of her, turning so he could face her head-on. One hand was dangerously close to touching her knee, the other on the coffee table. She could almost see him place his hands on her knees, slide up her thighs—

Concentrate, girl. He's going to say something.

"Look, I'm sorry I just tried to bail on you there. This has been a really awesome night. I'm glad I'm not wrecked in a ditch somewhere. I'd much rather be here with you." He paused but seemed to have more to say, so she waited. "And it's very generous of you to offer to have me back here."

"Not a big deal," she muttered.

"But look, I… I will admit I was nervous. Am nervous. Whatever. And I am maybe a bit confused. I don't want to make anything awkward between us. I have the utmost respect for you." He stopped for a moment. What was he thinking? What did any of that mean? Why was he even saying any of this? She could see the words running through his thoughts. "And… I also really, really want to kiss you right now. But only if you—"

She moved her right thigh out an inch, so that her leg touched his hand.

He stilled, eying her knee. "—want me to."

With her other foot, she pushed back the coffee table, risking sloshed wine everywhere but leaving more room in front of her. She paused, foot still propped high on the coffee table, legs parted before him.

There, was that any clearer? She had no idea how it looked to him, but to her it felt daring, brazen. Insanely bold. Terribly vulnerable.

He swallowed. She licked her lips, managing the slightest nod. His eyes darted down.

Without warning, his mouth covered hers, lips pressed gently for a moment, then harder, his beard scraping her skin. Oh, God, yes. His lips parted slightly, hot and wet. She followed his lead. And then his tongue was in her mouth, sweeping along her lip, plunging into her with greater and greater urgency. She clung to him, gripping his shoulders like a lifeline. His hand slid up her back, under her hair, and cradled her neck as he delved deeper into her mouth. So good, so great. She'd have gasped if she could have, but she was hardly even breathing at this point. His other hand ran up her thigh, gliding around her lower back, sweeping her hips forward and urging her closer to him. She scooted up to the edge, eager to feel his body against hers in more places than one.

Some incredulous part of her was shaking off the deep freeze and doing a happy dance. She had done it. Bring on the confetti, girls. Nick Markov was in her apartment.

And he was kissing her.

If this was possible, who knew what else the night could hold?

. . .

NICK MIGHT HAVE MISJUDGED her spot on the futon. And possibly her enthusiasm. As he tightened his arms around her, pulling her closer to him, she shifted forward eagerly. No longer frozen, apparently. The whole odd movement sent him off-balance and her practically off the couch on top of him.

He recovered before that could happen, but this was an awkward spot. He could only kiss her so long at this angle on his knees. He needed to either move beside her on the couch, move somewhere else entirely—dare he dream the bedroom?—or take advantage of this position and head south.

He had zero idea if she was interested in either of the latter two ideas, so he should start with the couch. A gentleman would.

Still, he delayed. Here her legs were spread around him, thighs pressing against his hips, and the whole lengths of their bodies molded together. Her soft curves pressed against his chest, and he didn't want to give up any of it. He ached to be as close to her as he possibly could, and he plunged his tongue further into her mouth, hungry, starving, desperate even. She hadn't moved much, but she seemed to be enjoying herself, clinging to him tightly and her tongue moving against his in a tentative caress.

Maybe… maybe he should try a different tack. He slid his hand from her hip down, slowly, toward her rear, giving her plenty of time to smack it away. She only kissed him harder. He gave her a tentative squeeze, urging her closer to him again.

A small squeak escaped from her, and he opened one eye, but she still seemed wholly engrossed in the kiss.

Time for the real test. Sliding up again, he found the edge of the white dress shirt and slid his fingers underneath, grazing the soft skin of her lower back.

She inhaled sharply but didn't pull away. No, in fact, her back arched beneath him. Her own hands seemed to remember themselves. They drifted down his chest toward his waist. His heart raced. Was this actually happening?

He was in Penny Collins's apartment, and she was kissing him. And reaching for the button on his jeans. This had to be a dream.

But in his dreams, her skin never felt quite this soft. He ran his hands up and down her back, trying to memorize the soft slide of her skin against this fingers, the temptation of her bra strap. She reached his belt and unbuckled it, then moved to the button on his jeans, but fumbled with it for a while. He would have smiled if he weren't kissing her, her awkwardness both sweet and electrifying. She clearly did not make a habit of inviting men back here, as many things had evinced throughout the night.

But she'd invited him.

Well, if she was going for the gold, so would he. He swept his hand up her rib cage and cupped her breast, savoring the slight roughness of lace under his hand. Of course she'd wear lace. Suddenly, he longed to see her. All of her. This had to be a dream. There was no way she would let him. This encounter was way over his level. She deserved way better than him.

But his hands had a mind of their own and reached for the sweet, small buttons on her shirt. Her own hands abandoned his pants and moved to help him, unbuttoning quickly, almost frantically. He moved to help her pull back the shirt, but she had already whipped it off, and his hands met only the smooth, naked skin of her shoulders.

Whoa, she was eager. Way more than he'd realized. Had she really had this in mind all along? When she'd suggested him staying over? Or was this just… impulsive?

It didn't matter. She was working on the buttons to his shirt now with more success. He needed to see her, sneak a peek of what they'd revealed. He broke away and moved his kiss down her jaw, then down her neck, stealing a long look at the pale pink of her bra and the curve of her breasts beneath it.

Pink and perfect. Of course.

She was making quick work of his shirt too, and suddenly her hands slid around his stomach and up his back, urging him closer to his surprise, and inadvertently driving the hard bulge in his pants into her hips. She let out a little gasp, and he smiled but tried to hide it in her hair, which smelled like a cupcake. Or maybe the whole apartment did.

There was a sweet, delicate innocence to her, in spite of her urgency. Hmm. He was likely more experienced than her. Maybe a lot more. Maybe he was not out-leveled after all.

Could it even be her first time? Well, he was just the man for the job. He'd be lying if he didn't admit he throbbed with need for her at the thought. Buttons on jeans weren't that hard to undo, were they?

Was this moving all way too fast?

He couldn't bring himself to care. Or stop. All the stars—and snow—had aligned today to bring them together here. He wasn't going to second-guess fate.

He shook his own shirt off now, tossing it aside, and her hands skimmed over his shoulders hungrily, down his arms, up his sides, and then again for another round. Memorizing him as well? The excitement, the reverence in it surprised him, almost as if she were savoring every moment of touching him. Pretty much nothing like having sex with Ashley. Whom he was definitely not going to think about again for the rest of the night.

He almost laughed as her hands slid down his back and slowed, hesitating. He hid his amusement in the crook of her neck as she sprinkled kisses across his shoulder, and sure enough, her hands drifted down now and grabbed his ass, ramming him against her again. Another breathless gasp. Finally for the first time tonight, one thing was clear. She definitely wanted this.

He kissed a gentle trail up to her earlobe, took it in his mouth, and sucked just for a second, earning a soft squeak. He straightened and whispered in her ear, "Do you want to go somewhere more comfortable, or are we doing this right here?"

She drew back sharply, eyes wide. Realizing just how far they'd been going? Having regrets? Please don't have regrets. But she seemed to relax when she caught sight of his smile. Nervous, he reminded himself. She's just nervous.

He shrugged, his hands still splayed across her lower back. "Unless you want to go back to watching the movie."

She looked at him like he was insane. Still not successfully forming words, she stood up. He stared up at her glorious form before taking her outstretched hand and rising.

His heart raced faster. He followed her to a dark room he presumed was her bedroom, snatching his bag on the way. As his eyes adjusted, yes, he could see a large bed to the left covered with pillows, a small end table and lamp, and a dresser to the right. And lots more unpacked boxes. The place was neat, if somewhat unlived in.

"Oh—wait, one second." She dropped his hand and dashed back into the living room.

He took the chance to pull the pack of condoms out of his bag —he was ever the optimist—and to throw the bag on the floor by the end table. He set the condoms cautiously by the lamp. Hopefully that wasn't too forward at this point. Penny did not seem like she'd have her own.

She came back with the pillow from the futon in one hand and two glasses of wine cradled skillfully in the other. She set the wine down next to the condoms, her eyes as round as the moon at the sight of them. She crawled onto the bed, sweeping all the fluffy pillows off the other side—a cloud and a rainbow went flying.

The view of her behind nearly drove him mad with desire. He ached to reach out and take her right there, but of course, it was too soon. Not for the first time. Especially not if it was her very first time.

No, not ever. Penny was too sweet, too good to want it rough. He pushed that darkness back down, but a knot of apprehension tightened in his stomach anyway. He'd bury that darkness forever if he could—what kind of person gets off on controlling the person they're supposed to love? But hating his darker urges had never made them go away.

He forgot all that, though, when she flopped over and looked at him, eyes hungrier now, hooded and smoky. Silver moonlight streaming in the window lit the edges of her shoulders and haloed her pale hair—gorgeous rim lighting that would make an amazing portrait, not that he was taking one or sharing this view with anyone else. Ever. He could just make out the curves of her breasts, the pale pink of her bra. Her long legs stretched out before him. He just looked at her for a moment, drinking her in.

She still had her socks on. Sky blue with smiling ice creams cones and cookies. Kawaii everywhere. Fucking adorable. Gently, he lifted her right foot, stroking the sole as he slowly took off one sock, then switching to the other foot. Her leg trembled beneath his fingers.

Setting her foot back on the bed, he ran his hands up her calves, nudging her legs apart. Making room for him. She shook again beneath him as he knelt onto the bed, crawling his way on hands and knees over her, until his face was barely an inch from hers. His thigh nestled against the heat between her legs.

He kissed her softly again before she collapsed off her elbows and back on the bedspread, her breaths warm and quick. Her hands reached for his forearms now, ran up him, eyes searching. Memorizing, he thought. Just like he was. Trying to capture this moment and never forget it.

"Pen, are you sure you want to do this?"

"Yes," she breathed. "Very."

She swallowed and brushed some hair back off her face. He waited a moment longer, hoping to stave off any regrets that might be lurking.

"Very sure," she said as he continued his vigil. She opened her mouth again, hesitated, but then seemed to muster her courage. "I mean,… I guess you should know… I'm not very experienced."

He smiled, drifting closer to her, letting their chests brush as he kissed her shoulder, shifting down to her cleavage to ease the tension in them both. "I gathered that," he whispered against the pale lace.

"You did?" She didn't sound too happy about that.

"That's why I asked." He kissed the edge of the bra tenderly, wondering if this was the wrong time to yank it down and take her nipple in his mouth. Probably.

"What if I told you I'm like… really, really not very experienced?"

"Is this your first time, Pen?" He ran his tongue under the edge of her bra, kneading her gently with his fingers.

She shivered, then nodded and bit her lip in that way that made him want to bury himself inside her and never look back. "Yeah."

He forced his restraint, his mind back to her and what she was feeling. "Are you cold? What is it? Should we get under the covers?"

"No, I just—I mean, yeah, let's get under the covers. But I just like it when you call me that."

He smiled, then reached over and pulled the covers down. She moved toward them, but he caught her by the waistband. "Wait. Let's take care of these first." Relenting and smiling herself now, she lay back as he unbuttoned her trousers and pulled them and her panties down in one smooth motion. Another soft gasp. He hoped it were more of the delighted than terrified variety.

Then he gazed at her lovely form on the bed while he unbuttoned his own pants and dropped them, kicking his boxers off. As they fell, she propped herself up on her elbows again. Trying to get a better look? He smirked, but then tried to hide it. There wasn't much spectacular about his lanky, geeky frame to get a look at.

He pulled the covers down further and climbed in, and she slipped in beside him. His mouth met hers as his fingers went for the one remaining obstacle—the bra clasp. His erection was hard as hell by now and pressed insistently and rather rudely into her leg. Hopefully she didn't mind.

The bra came free, and she wriggled around until it was extricated. He tossed it aside, sweeping her against him, reveling in the smooth warmth of her skin against his.

"Still sure, Pen?" he whispered against her mouth.

"Hell yes," she whispered back.

He grinned. "Okay, well, if you're sure, you just keep telling me when you like it, and when you don't, and we'll be fine."

"That sounds easier said than done."

"Practice makes perfect, right?"

"What?"

"Well, we'll just have to practice. A lot."

She burst out laughing. Before she could even stop, he scooted rapidly under the covers, calling, "First lesson!"

"What?"

She seemed legitimately unsure of what he was going to do, especially given the gasp as his nose nuzzled into the hair between her legs. He ran his fingers over her soft center and restrained himself from thrusting a finger straight into her when he discovered her wet center. She might be inexperienced, but her body certainly knew what it was doing.

And so did he. Thanks to she-who-would-not-be-named.

He pressed his tongue into her first, then slid up to her clit. Her thighs tightened around him, squeezing, up over his shoulders, and she let out a quiet moan. He traced his fingers up her thigh, then over her center while he thrust his tongue into her core, setting off more startled noises. Then he switched, licking and sucking at her clit while he slid one finger inside her.

The groan that escaped her was heavenly, and he shuddered at the sound of it. He wanted to surge up and fuck her brains out right now, not wait a second longer. But no, no way, chances were she wouldn't come that way, not the first time, and he was making her come tonight. What if he never got another chance? He wasn't getting anything until she'd had her fill at least once. First things first. He was going to do this right.

He stroked his finger in and out of her, sucking and licking, until finally he thought he just might be able to fit a second one. She gasped again, louder, and damn was she tight around him. He watched her face as best he could, the white light of the moon outside limning her cute features, her closed eyes, her heaving chest. God, he wanted to see her come. It wasn't just for her sake anymore.

He twisted his hand around and curved his fingers up, feeling for the spot. Her eyes snapped open, her mouth dropping open without a sound. This was his chance. Speeding up, he buried his face in her delicious taste, the sounds of her pleasure filling his ears. Her hands had a death grip on the pillows behind her head, her eyes squeezed shut again, and then—

Her thighs tightened around his head as she gasped and cried out, her back arching and hips bucking into him, and it was all he could do to hold on, to finish the job, to not shove his cock inside her and fuck her senseless right there. Oh, but in a minute or two.

She wouldn't know what hit her. Her movements slowed, then stopped, and she reached for him instead of the sheets.

He happily dove back up into her arms, and she pulled his head against her, down onto her shoulder. Sweat slicked them both, and she was panting even harder than he was. His cock throbbed against her again, but he ignored it for a moment, relishing the feel of their bodies simply lying side by side.

"How's that for dessert, huh? Better than brownies?" he said, kissing her skin just because it was there.

She laughed breathlessly. "Maybe just a little."

"I'm still hoping for brownies, though." Still in her arms, he could reach her nipple if he just scooted down a little and… He ran his tongue around it.

She drew back, giggling, but he would not be deterred so easily. He took it into his mouth and sucked, nipping at her gently, and she squirmed and swatted him again. "That tickles!"

Laughing, he settled for a moment with his face between her breasts. This right here. This might be heaven.

"Nick?"

"Yeah?" He shut his eyes, listening to her voice reverberate through her chest, her heartbeat, her breathing.

"What about you?"

"I'm in no hurry." He smiled against her even though she couldn't see him.

She was quiet for a moment, running her hands up and down his back. A little more restless than before. He might not be, but maybe she was?

"Take me, Nick."

He jerked his head up in surprise, meeting her gaze.

"Take me. Now." He stared for a moment, savoring those words, those sweet lips. "Please?" she whispered, and he almost came on her leg just at that. Trembling at those words, he took her lips with his again for a long, hard kiss, then reached for the condoms.

Rolling one on as quickly as humanly possible, he cursed himself for letting himself get so turned on. He needed all the control he could muster for this. Lowering himself back over her, he paused. "It might hurt. Do you want it fast or slow?"

She hesitated, then shrugged, squeezing his forearms. "I want you like yesterday."

He laughed. "Fast then?"

"Yes, please."

There was that delicious word again. His kink might be showing. Shuddering and barely holding it together, he nodded and centered himself against her, then lowered his lips to meet hers. Sliding his tongue into her mouth, he thrust into her body, wet heat engulfing him.

This gasp put all the others to shame. But not too much pain creased her brow. When she'd relaxed, he kissed her again, not moving. "Okay?" he whispered. He was barely okay. He needed a minute probably more than she did, her body firm yet yielding to him, throwing him to the very edge of control.

She nodded. "Okay. Good, in fact. Not as good as the other dessert, but you know, not everything can be brownies."

Laughing, he lowered his mouth to hers again, daring to slide just a little out of her, then ram back in again. And then again, a little farther out this time. Maybe he should be more gentle. He broke away from the kiss, studying her face for a hint of tension, but there was none. Her eyes were closed, lost in feeling.

Straightening up so he could watch her face, he allowed himself to move in her faster now. God, of all the men, Penny wanted him. Had chosen him for this moment. Even if it all fell to pieces tomorrow, this would be something she would never forget. And neither would he.

Her hands tightened around his forearms, then drifted up to his shoulders and back down again, her simple caress sending waves of pleasure through his shoulders and back. He was going to make damn sure this didn't fall apart, though. He didn't just want this, he wanted everything. This a thousand times, a thousand tomorrows. She was his someone, and if he could help it, he was never going to let her go. If he could ever afford a damn fireplace, he wanted

Penny to be the one with him beside it. Preferably exactly like this at least some of the time.

A groan escaped his lips as her legs crushed harder around him, somewhere between ecstasy and urgency, and he drove into her with abandon now, no sign to slow down playing across her sweet eyes, her panting lips. Her eyes popped open, and to his surprise, her body quaked around his, trembling and clenching around him in pulsing waves. A cry slipped from her, propelling him over the edge after her into delirious bliss, his own shout of release following her own.

He collapsed against her, propped on his elbows, and just listened to their breathing for a moment. Smelled her skin, her shampoo. Felt her soft hair tickling his face. He slid out after a long moment of procrastination. Panting, he raised his head to look at her. "Good?" he choked out between gasps. "You okay?"

She grinned. "Way better than brownies."

"I'll have to actually have some to judge that." He grinned back and pressed a closemouthed kiss against her as her hands cradled his face. "Where's your bathroom again? I'll be right back."

She pointed. He left her as briefly as he could and clambered back into her arms, breathing her in again.

In spite of himself, his shoulders tensed a little. He clung tighter to her in response. This was always when shit got weird with Ashley —well, if it hadn't been weird to begin with, which it usually was. But this was the moment she would always get up and go do something ridiculous, like run the dishwasher or start reading a damn book. Or banish him to the couch. Why had he ever put up with that? She had never, ever lay beside him for more than a few moments, as long as he could remember.

Penny's not Ashley, he reminded himself. And he was not thinking about that crazy bitch again. He pushed her from his mind and kissed Penny's shoulder.

She sighed and squirmed closer to him. For one horrible moment, he thought she might break away, but instead she shifted down, putting her head on his shoulder, tossing her arm around his waist, and pulling him in. He kissed the top of her head and just lay there, listening to her breath. The snowed-in city was especially silent tonight. His eyes traced the curve of her hip under the sheets, wanting to run his hands all over her again, but he had a sneaking suspicion she was almost asleep. The air was sweet with the smell of sex and baked goods and Penny.

Looked like all that snow shoveling had been worth it, to say the least. He squeezed her closer and drifted off to sleep.

Chapter 6

THE NEXT MORNING, Penny opened her eyes to the sound of the door buzzer ringing. She sat bolt upright, even more confused when she remembered she was naked. Snatching the covers over her, to her shock she heard Nick's voice from the hall, buzzing someone in.

For a foggy moment, her pulse raced. Wait, what had happened last night?

Whoa, what had she been *thinking*? She had barely talked to Nick for two hours in total, and then she'd thrown caution into the incinerator and let him in, pretty much as far as she could possibly let anyone in. Who the hell was he letting into her apartment? What if he was a psycho? What if he was—

Someone knocked, and the door opened. "Fifteen forty-five," a voice said from the hall.

"Here you go," said Nick.

What the hell? Still, her pulse slowed as the night slowly came back to her. Every glorious moment, every shadowed touch, those peaks of sheer intensity she'd barely dreamed of when her own fingers did the walking. He had been nothing but sweet and gentle and kind.

Sir Dreamy to the core. Better than she'd imagined him.

She took a deep breath. It was fine. She just wasn't used to waking up next to someone. Or waking up to them letting someone into her living room, either.

On the end table, his phone buzzed, and she glanced at it automatically. And froze.

It was a text from Ashley, for fuck's sake. *Hey stud, why didn't you text me back last night?*

She tore her eyes away, a small part of her filled with a sudden smug satisfaction that for once someone had ignored Ashley in favor of her. Ugh, what a terrible thought. But other paranoid thoughts raced through her mind. She hadn't specifically *asked* him if he was single. Available. Or if he wanted a relationship. Maybe this was just a one-night stand to him. Maybe he just wanted another fuck buddy.

Like Ashley had been.

Oh, God. She wanted so much more than that. She ran a panicked hand through her hair, trying to force her brain awake. And to think. To be rational. Deep breaths. It could be nothing. Sir Dreamy wouldn't be very chivalrous if he just slept around, right? Okay, sure, she didn't know for sure either way, he had never claimed to be chivalrous, but… it didn't feel right. He really seemed like he'd been into her. God, let her not be being super, *super* naive. This is what she got for dodging the hard conversations and jumping in headfirst.

She slipped out of bed and winced. Some muscles she wasn't used to using were quite stretched. Holy hell. Straightening, she considered putting on pajamas, but a part of her had kind of hoped if she put them on, they'd be taken off again soon. Maybe just a robe.

Feeling brazen, and possibly insane, she eschewed her fluffy pink slippers and strode barefoot and naked under her robe out into the hall.

He turned from the kitchen. He had his jeans on, but no shirt, looking a little sheepish and a lot hot. He was pale as hell; was it odd that that seemed super hot for no reason she could explain? Her eyes couldn't resist raking down his long, lean lines, following the trail of brown fuzz leading from his navel down into his pants, drawing her eye ever downward. She forced her gaze up to his smile and away from his package. Two take-out containers sat on the counter. "Hey," he said softly. "Buzzer wake you up?" He held out his arms, beckoning her.

She nodded, smiling and heading for him. She was such a sucker, but she wanted her body against his again, doing whatever activity he pleased. Hugging would suffice.

"Sorry, I didn't realize it'd be so loud." He grinned. "But I heard you get takeout from this Eden place and that you like strawberry French toast."

He opened one container, and her eyebrows shot up. "You got delivery from Eden? For *breakfast?*"

"Yeah," he said slowly, as if he wasn't sure her exclamation was positive or negative.

"That's amazing!" She seized the box and darted toward her dining table.

He laughed, grabbing his to follow her. "I couldn't figure out your newfangled coffee maker. And I was hoping to bring these back to you on plates. In bed. But you know, things didn't go according to plan." He eyed the table with a slight frown for a moment as he sat down. Did he think he recognized it? It'd been in her and Ashley's apartment forever.

She grinned as she ripped off a piece with her fingers and stuffed it in her mouth. "This is perfect. I'll turn on the coffee. Go ahead and eat. What did you get?"

"Guess."

"Lemon pancakes."

"You were paying attention."

"So were you, clearly. Hazelnut, chocolate, or dark roast?"

"Dark roast."

"I figured." She hit the button, and the coffee maker hissed to life. "Milk and sugar?"

"Just milk. These pancakes have enough sugar for the entire day."

She made herself a hazelnut and joined him back at the table.

She'd scarfed down one of the four pieces before she remembered the text from stupid Ashley. "So…" she said, trying to sound super casual. It was maybe working. "I should probably have asked you this last night, but you are single, right?" She winced at how that came out. Way too judgmental. If he wasn't, she only had herself to blame for not clarifying—

His eyes widened. "Why? Wait, let me guess." He jumped up, headed into the bedroom, and returned with his phone, holding it up with a question in his eyes.

She blushed. "I wasn't trying to look at it. It just popped up where I sit my phone sometimes—"

"It's fine, you can look at it. Listen, I cut things off with this girl *three* months ago. She won't stop texting me."

That did sound like Ashley. Hard to shake. Sounded like he hadn't quite completed the process. "Maybe you should block her," Penny muttered, and then reeled at her own suggestion. He should probably know Penny knew Ashley before taking any suggestions like that from her.

"You know, you're probably right." He didn't seem at all fazed by the idea. He read out loud as he typed in a reply. "Stop—texting —me—I—told—you—it's—over. There. Think that will work?"

"Probably not."

He grinned and took another bite, and then to her surprise, he turned the phone around and showed her that he'd typed what he'd said. "Oh wait, I know." He snatched it back, and his fingers flying, then turned the phone back around to her.

An unsent message was waiting in the input field: *I'm dating someone else, leave me alone.*

"Would that be fair to say?" He smiled crookedly.

"Oh, yes, I suppose," she said, her tone faux casual. Her grin betrayed her. Heat flushed through her again, not from embarrassment this time. For once.

Dating someone else. Dating *her*.

"Sent!" He tossed the phone aside and took another bite of pancake. If he was trying to look done with Ashley, he was sure succeeding. Of course, three months was a long time. He probably really was over her. And those were just the kinds of texts Ashley would send.

And whatever, who cared about that ancient history? Nick Markov had just told someone he was dating her! Penny Collins! Insanity!

She needed to text Anka. But it would probably be rude while Nick was still there. Especially because she did not want him to see whatever crazy things Anka would say. Maybe she'd sneak off to the bathroom. Maybe she'd be *really* wild and not even text her until he left.

And who knew when that would be!

"Any word on the snow outside?"

He frowned, looking out the window. "It's melting at a rather dramatic clip."

"Damn. Now I guess you'll have to come up with a new excuse to stay over."

He grinned like a fool. "I can think of one."

"But will I go for it?" She smiled slyly.

"You went for it twice last night," he said, laughing. "I'm optimistic about my chances."

"True, true. And now you've plied me with French toast."

"I hope this coffee doesn't mean we can't get back in bed."

"Oh, no. It definitely doesn't. I didn't even put on pajamas."

"I'm counting on that next then." He took a sip, "Wait—what?" His eyes strayed down her throat and chest, then snapped back up. He gulped.

"Oh, nothing." She blushed again. "Do you have anywhere to be soon?" How much longer could this heaven last?

"I can stay past lunch, if that's what you're asking."

"Ooh. Brownies. Yes."

"But I do have work tonight."

"Work?" How did that even work for a photographer?

"Weddings are primarily in the summer, so I have a part-time gig keeping my friend's gallery open. There's a wine walk or something."

"Oh, that could be worse. Where is it?"

"Yeah, it's not flipping burgers. It's in Doll Town. So I take over for him at like six. But I guess I should probably run home and shower first."

You could shower here, she thought. She stayed silent, not quite able to bring herself to suggest it yet.

"So we have till maybe four? What about you?"

"What time even is it?"

He glanced at his phone. "Ten fifteen."

She slapped a palm to her forehead. This was a *Thursday*, for God's sake. "I totally forgot. I have class in fifteen minutes."

He jumped forward. "You need to go?"

"No, forget it. I'll just skip it."

"No way, we can—"

She waved it off. "It's fine. I can blame the snow. I know the material anyway. The buses can't get me there in time, even if they're running."

"I could drive you—"

"Next time," she said, shaking her head.

He stopped and relaxed back into his seat. "If you're sure."

"This doesn't happen every day, you know. I think I will survive one missed class."

"Do you have others later?"

"Not until five. Night classes today. Terrible schedule, I know."

"So… we have all day almost."

She grinned at him. "Yeah, we do. We could almost watch the rest of the *Lord of the Rings*."

"If you didn't have the extended editions."

"Perceptive."

"I try. Did you really watch any of it last night? I know I wasn't paying much attention."

She snorted. "I've seen it a zillion times, but yeah, I was not super interested in the movie."

"What could possibly have been so distracting?"

She made a face at him, then rose to take the rest of her food and put it in the fridge. She didn't want to be too full if there were… activities other than movies to come. When she returned to the table, he snagged her around the waist and pulled her close.

"What's this I hear about no pajamas?" He tugged playfully on the belt of the robe as he studied her eyes.

She tugged the belt the rest of the way and let the robe fall open. Again, it felt daring, brazen, possibly insane. But what did she have to hide from him? She had nothing she wanted to hide. And she wanted more of everything they had together.

He swallowed as his hand slipped inside her robe, fingers trailing along her waist, as soft and thrilling as a paintbrush whispering across her skin. His gaze raked down her body. "I think I'm ready to get back in bed."

"Ditto."

NICK DROPPED Penny off at class and arrived for the wine walk with fifteen minutes to spare. Carl had the place lit up, polished, and raring to go, and now it was just up to Nick to make sure none of the half-drunk members of the local community destroyed anything.

He sank into the leather chair at the attendant's desk and dropped his car keys on the leather blotter, eying them for a moment. Bob had claimed they'd turned up under the couch after all, even though Nick could have sworn he'd looked under there. But Bob had cheerfully handed them over the minute he and Penny had arrived… well into the afternoon.

The rabbit's foot mocked him. He shook his head. Maybe not so unlucky after all.

He dropped his keys in his coat pocket, very deliberately this time, and zipped the pocket closed over them before shrugging out of his coat and scanning the current state of the gallery. Three patrons wandered, small plastic tumblers of wine in hand. None looked particularly out of place or clumsy, and all looked sincerely interested, so he leaned back in his chair, relaxing a little.

The collection in Carl's gallery was more on the "eclectic" side, or so Nick liked to think of it. It wasn't the sort of place where a sparse expanse of bamboo flooring was surrounded by picture after picture spaced across perfect white. No, the place was a warm cave filled with treasures, the walls pleasantly bathed in navy, gray, and other shades of blue, complementing the nature photography and the glass sculpture. Other art, both two- and three-dimensional, created a sort of confused maze through the place. Nick wasn't sure if this was intentional so that the patrons would get lost and look at more pieces on the way through, or if Carl simply didn't know how to organize so many pieces any better.

Either way, the forest of artwork camouflaged the attendant's desk, off to the side and rather invisible to new visitors, which conveniently allowed him to watch them without being super obvious about it. It also kept many people from making small talk and left him to his own devices—beyond making sure no one knocked anything over or stole anything. Rarely, someone asked him a price. Even more rarely, someone actually bought something.

This left him sitting in peace, wondering just how those keys had disappeared since he *never* lost his keys, until the door chimed. Another lone patron was on her way in.

Ashley.

He ran his hand through his hair, rubbed his forehead, and braced himself for whatever bullshit was to come as she wended her way through the labyrinth of artwork toward him.

"Nick! Fancy seeing you here." She smiled wickedly as she took a sip of wine. Her short, crimson fingernails tapped the plastic glass of merlot and swirled it idly. A plaid flannel shirt matched the cherry of her lips and the black of her usual leather boots. That was Ash—passionate, bold, with an edge of darkness always.

He rolled his eyes. "I'm working, Ash. Don't distract me."

She glanced around. "You're right. That little old lady definitely looks like a bull in a china shop. Better keep an eye on *her*. So you're dating someone?"

"Yeah." He sighed—and trained his eyes on the older woman, if only for somewhere *else* to look.

"Who?"

"None of your business, Ash."

"What, I can't be happy for you? Congratulate you?"

"Is that what you're doing? I think you can do that without knowing who."

"Are you ashamed of her or something?"

He leveled a withering glare at her. "You're such a conniving bitch sometimes. Have I told you that?"

She gave him a look of mock shock, one hand splayed across her chest. "Nick. The things you say to the woman who taught you everything you know. Did you show her some of our tricks?" She winked as she took another sip.

He shook his head. He was *never* going to taint Penny, even if he himself hadn't escaped it. The devilish amusement in Ash's eyes hardened his resolve to keep it all locked away.

"Really? Why hold back?"

Because she's sweet and innocent and nothing like you, he wanted to shout. But that would give Ash too much power. He was learning. He had to tell her as little as possible.

But the hesitation and his automatic glare told her enough. "Holy shit. You're dating a *vanilla* chick, aren't you?"

"Get out of here, Ash. You're disturbing the customers." And him.

She shook her head. "It'll never last, man. You're gonna get bored of her."

Not likely. "You don't even know her. How can you try to convince me I'm going to get bored? I just told you we were dating. Why would you assume we've even had sex?" He struggled to lower his voice, but the harsh whisper only drew the little old lady's raised eyebrows. He gave her his best smile and a wave, and she turned her wide eyes back to a large color print of sunset over the Rockies.

Ash snickered. "I assume because I know you, Nick. If there's even a remote chance, you go for it."

He strove to ignore her, even as the knot in his stomach tightened further. Wasn't that exactly what he'd done last night? He was *not* admitting she might be right, but she did know him. Better than Penny did. Was she right? Would he really get bored? He shuddered at the thought, then glanced at her.

She was smirking. Damn it, she knew that had gotten under his skin. "Okay, I'm gonna have to guess until you tell me who it is."

"This is not twenty questions. I don't have to tell you anything."

She tapped her finger to pursed lips, the gesture somehow mocking. "That dark-room chick. Wendy."

"Fuck off, Ash."

"That study partner you had, what was her name, Emily?"

He checked over each patron to make sure she hadn't kept him from noticing something was amiss. Did she really have this checklist of women he had ever associated with? He hadn't kept track of the other dudes she'd fucked around with. He didn't know who they were, nor did he want to.

"Oh, I know. That model you liked. Gabrielle?"

He glared at her. "Gabrielle is engaged. And we only worked together for one portraits class."

"Angela."

"Who?"

"That barista we always talked to. Apparently not. Wait, I've got it. Amber Parsons. She was hot."

"What? Wendy's friend?"

"Yeah. She's a photog chick, too, isn't she?"

"Amber is gay, Ash."

"Oh." Ashley scowled, folding her arms across her chest. "Well, fuck. Maybe you actually went out and tried to meet someone, like a normal person. Next thing I know, you'll be telling me it's fucking Penny Collins or someone ridiculous like that."

He froze.

"Wait—oh my God. It *is* Penny? Are you serious?"

He narrowed his eyes at her but didn't deny it. Too late now, apparently. He braced himself. He had no idea how Ash would handle him actually being with someone else—in spite of the fact they'd never been exclusive—but she probably wouldn't handle it well. She was the one who'd taken advantage of their unique arrangement. He never had. He was pretty sure neither of them had been doing the "open" thing the way you were supposed to.

"You're dating my old roommate? Wow. Very unoriginal, Nick, jeez."

He ducked his head, hoping to hide his wide eyes. Penny was Ashley's old roommate? What the hell? They knew each other? And Penny hadn't mentioned it?

"If you're just looking for a blonder version of me, I assure you, she's not it."

"I am well aware of that." He glared at her now. "Keep out of it, Ashley. Or I swear to God—"

She smirked again. "Or you'll what?" She leaned forward over the desk, showcasing her cleavage. He rolled the chair backward and tensed, considering bolting outright. "Or you'll tell her all the things you did to me? Or even better, what I did to you?" She grinned wickedly and raised an eyebrow. "Or maybe I should do that!"

Inwardly, he winced. How could he scare her away from talking to Penny? He groped and came up with nothing. He had no leverage, because what did Ash care about? Very little. Natural one, critical fail.

"I can't believe it. You're dating fucking rainbows-puppies-and-sunshine Penny. Why don't you just defile a Care Bear while you're at it?"

"Shut the fuck up, Ashley," he whispered, even surprising himself at the coldness in his voice. "Don't you dare talk to her about this. Leave us alone."

"Or what?" She smirked again.

"Or I'll never speak to you again," he said slowly. A weak threat, but it was all he had.

She pouted. "Heaven forbid." But something about the gesture was off. Put-on, maybe. Even if she didn't want to show it, his threat had gotten to her. At least a little.

"I'm serious, Ash. Stay away from her. And me. The past is in the past."

She shook her head, more serious now. "Whatever. When you're ready for a real woman, Nick Markov, I'll be here to pick up the pieces." And then she turned on her booted heel and walked out.

Chapter 7

OHMYGAWD. You're dating Nick Markov? You lucky slut.

Well. That sure livened up the history of auditing fraud. Penny crammed the phone back into her pocket, chiding herself for looking during class. But she'd hoped it'd been something nice. From Nick. She certainly hadn't expected her ex-roomie. How the hell could Ashley have found out? If she hadn't found out from Penny…

It must have been from Nick.

Shit. What had Ash told him? She should've admitted she knew Ashley when she had the chance. She pulled the phone back out and stared at the words.

At that same moment, Ashley texted again. *So did he pop your cherry yet or what?*

Penny's stomach dropped, and her cheeks flushed hot. Yeah, *that* wasn't getting an answer. And she needed to stop looking at her phone.

God, Nick was going to think Penny was a stalker. And break up with her psycho ass pronto.

Ash had probably told him every embarrassing story she could think of. Not that there was very much to tell, but Ashley had never understood Penny's love for all things cute, adorable, and cuddly. Penny had never done things like get drunk and vomit all over Ashley's bed or something—unlike her more adventurous roommate. But they had very different definitions of "embarrassing." What had she ever been thinking to agree to move in with Ashley? She sighed, and the blond girl beside her glanced at her in annoyance. Penny blushed further.

How had she and Ash ever been friends? People could change a hell of a lot in four years.

She threw the phone in her bag and tried to focus on class.

The lecture droned on for another hour before people started packing up their things, and Penny finally retrieved the phone from her bag with dread. A handful of texts waited.

Ashley: *Are you gonna spill about freaky with Markov's chains or am I going to have to come over there?*

Ashley: *Harrr-harrr-harrr puns are amazing, I'm so brilliant, wouldn't you agree*

Ashley: *We should have a drink. Celebrate. Call me.*

Penny rolled her eyes. That sounded like a trap and a half. And drinking was Ashley's thing. Penny still had no idea how to respond, other than to blush furiously. There were other, better texts, though.

Nick: *Sushi Friday?*

Penny grinned down at her phone in spite of herself. Whatever Ashley had said, she liked his reaction. But that wasn't all.

Nick: *I forgot to say I'm done at 10*

Nick: *Want to do something later? Is that too late? You probably have class in the morning, you shouldn't skip this time. But I'd love to see you*

Nick: *Am I supposed to be playing it cooler than this? ;)*

She checked the time. Eight o'clock, a bit earlier than usual for class to end. Plenty of time for baking. She unlocked the phone and typed quickly. *Class just finished. Meet at my place? Or yours? Or did you want to go out?*

Nick: *I'll go wherever you want me.*

She grinned like an idiot, then stifled it when she realized her professor was eying her. Probably because she was the last one still sitting down. *My apartment. I'll have brownies.*

Nick: *I have high expectations for these brownies.*

I'm not intimidated. Do you like peanut butter? She couldn't suppress her grin as she threw her things into her bag and hurried out.

ANOTHER TEXT from Ashley arrived just as she opened the door for Nick. God, get a life, girl. She glared at the phone as Nick shucked off his coat and boots. Ashley was getting desperate now. *C'mon! I want details details details! Don't make me try to get them from Anka.* As if Anka would spill the beans. *She* knew better than that.

"What is it?" he said, noticing her glare.

Fuck. How to handle this... She took a deep breath, thinking of how he'd shown her his phone so casually. She swallowed hard and held hers out. "It appears you may have run into a mutual acquaintance of ours?"

He read for a moment, then glared darkly at the phone. She'd never seen his face quite that dark. Her pulse quickened. God. This was it. He'd conclude she was a weird stalker any second now. Probably because she kind of *was* a weird stalker. She'd felt so calm at the end of class, so sure it didn't matter, but that was before she'd seen that expression on his face.

Was it weird to hope for a goodbye screw, even if she knew it was over? Was that slutty? It was probably slutty.

Who the hell cared! If she only got two days with Nick Markov, she'd take whatever screwing she could get.

"So... you know Ashley?" he said slowly, handing her the phone back.

Penny ducked her head, blushing as she skittered away toward the kitchen. He followed her. "Yeah."

He stopped and raised his eyebrows at the brownie dish on the stove, steam rising cheerily from the shiny, chocolaty goodness. "Wow, that was fast. Maybe we should talk about this over brownies?" he said, one corner of his mouth lifting.

"Okay!" At least that meant he wasn't bolting just yet. Or angry. She levered one out of the pan and onto a plate. "Here you go. Dark chocolate peanut butter with ganache."

He stared at it for a second. Crap, was there something wrong with it? Maybe he was allergic—no, she'd asked, but— Just before she blurted out her fears, he looked up, and the smile he gave her melted her in place, a complicated expression she couldn't quite read. But definitely a good one.

"You want some milk?" Oh hell, that was so kindergarten of her. "Or coffee or tea?"

"I'll take a coffee if you don't mind. Please."

"Sure!" she said, chipper as a chipmunk. She forced herself to take a deep breath. Even under the shadow of the conversation they needed to have, it was still delightful to have Sir Dreamy in her kitchen, being all polite and small smiles and tall confidence. She urged him and his brownie to a seat at the table, then scampered back into the kitchen and started up a dark roast.

"She stopped by the gallery," he called through the pass-through, over the sound of the machine brewing. The heavenly scent filled the air.

"Oh." She was glad he couldn't see the sigh of relief she heaved. How had he known she'd want to hear that? "That must have been fun."

He laughed—actually laughed. The tension in her shoulders eased. "She interrogated me. For what it's worth, I never gave you up."

She returned with the coffee, frowning. "I'm not sure I follow."

"She asked who I was dating. I told her to fuck off. But she actually guessed."

"She… guessed?" Penny blinked and then tried to hide her surprise with a huge bite of her own brownie. That seemed impossible. She was sure Ash had never suspected that Penny had a thing for Nick. Or that Nick wasn't just a faceless man in Ash's parade of men.

"Well, she guessed a whole list of people, and she was muttering that it definitely couldn't be you, and I accidentally gave it away. I didn't realize she knew you, so she caught me by surprise."

"You… didn't want her to know?"

He reached forward and caught her elbow. "It's not like that,

Pen. It's just none of her business. I want her to leave you alone. And me alone. Us alone."

Us. Her heart fluttered, and she couldn't help but smile. "Guess *that* didn't work."

"Yeah, she probably texted you the minute she walked away. I don't want her causing trouble or trying to screw this up."

Her eyes widened at his phrasing—that was intense commitment for having first spoken just two days ago—but he didn't seem to notice.

He shook his head and took a bite, savoring it as his eyes closed. "Jesus Christ, Penny, these are heaven."

She flushed with pleasure, squirming around in her seat, definitely thinking about something other than brownies with that expression on his face. He didn't seem mad. Maybe they would make it through this conversation after all. "We were roommates." She ducked her head.

"Oh, yeah?"

"For three and a half years."

His eyes widened. "Wow. So you're close?"

"No. Not anymore. We were friends as freshmen. Total mistake on my part. We're pretty different, if you hadn't noticed."

"I definitely noticed." He raised the brownie to get a better look at it. "She never made me brownies, that's for sure."

"I knew I needed to move out after the first year, but I never got it together. Or found another roommate. My best friend, Anka, lives with her boyfriend, so she wasn't an option. I knew Ash and I would grow even farther apart now that she's graduated and I'm not. So I decided it was time to finally bite the bullet and move out."

"Wow, so… I mean, I dated Ashley for almost three years too. Sort of. We weren't exclusive. But it was the same time you lived there. So we were in the same apartment how often and we didn't even know it?"

Penny winced. Oh she'd known it; he was the oblivious one. She had wanted to tell him in some other way, something sweet, over pillow talk, a moment that would make her seem less stalkery. But not coming clean right now would be even worse. "Actually, *I* kind of knew…" She ducked her head again. She was probably red as a beet now.

He cocked his head, smiling. "Wait, what?"

She nodded. "She used to post photos of you on Facebook, and I used to see you asleep on the couch. Why were you always on the couch instead of in her room?"

He waved it off, that dark expression drifting over his face again. "Long and terrible story. How did we not meet, then?"

"Oh, I always hid in my room. Some of her guys freaked me out. And if you can believe it, I used to be even more shy."

He smiled. "I can believe it. I used to be too."

A silence settled, and she relaxed a little more. There. She was off the hook and didn't even sound like a stalker. Hallelujah! Although she had somehow avoided the real kicker of admitting how she'd admired him from afar all that time.

"Well, I'm glad Uncle Bob and D&D finally brought us together." He took a sip of coffee. "You really should play next time, you know. You want to make a character this weekend?"

Warmth flushed through her, and she couldn't help herself. She darted over to him and wrapped her arms around his neck. He slid the chair back and pulled her down into his lap, locking his lips with hers as she squeaked in surprise. His tongue swirled against hers, his taste exquisite, all chocolate and coffee and memories of the night before.

No. This was a distraction. She hadn't really come *entirely* clean, and when would she get the courage to if not now? She should explain it all. Leave nothing more to worry about.

Their lips parted, leaving her breathless. He nuzzled her neck, nipped at her shoulder. "We could make you a character right now, if *that's* how you feel about it."

His hair was soft against her cheek and smelled like her shampoo. "Nick, you should know, uh…"

"Yes? You've secretly already got a character made and waiting in the wings?" His breath was hot on her neck, his voice rich with laughter, and she smothered a giggle of her own. He pulled away and cocked his head to the side, smiling. "Because that would be hot."

"You should know I kinda had a crush on you even back then." She winced and braced herself for his reaction, biting her lip.

"What!" His eyebrows shut up. The hand that circled her waist held her tight as iron against him.

She was blushing furiously now. "Am I red as an apple?"

"No. You're much prettier than an apple. It's more like a strawberry."

She swatted at him.

"And here I thought I was the one who liked you first."

Her eyes widened. "You did? When? I thought maybe…" She glanced away.

"You thought that this hadn't occurred to me before last night?"

"Yeah," she admitted.

"Oh, no, no, no." He laughed. "I told you. Only idiots go out in snowstorms like that. And people with incentives."

"You came to see me?"

"You hadn't gathered that by now?"

Well, now that he put it *that* way. "I… had no idea. I mean, it occurred to me, but I didn't believe it. Wait, wait, how long, then?"

"Basically right away. Well, as far as *I* knew. I noticed you the first time I came to visit Bob at the center. But I couldn't get up the nerve to talk to you."

"You mean, *I* couldn't get up the nerve to talk to *you*."

"No, really. I couldn't either."

"I find it hard to believe anyone who dated Ashley could be shy," she said. He glanced away, eyes dark and brow furrowed. "Shit. Sorry. I mean… I just always assume I'm the only socially awkward one."

"You're not." He pressed a quick kiss to her mouth. "It's adorable when you do it, though."

She blushed. "No, it's not."

"To me it is. You're right, though. I was more shy before I dated Ash. But I'm still pretty quiet."

"You pulled it together all right. Once I tripped and nearly killed you."

"May I remind you *you're* the one who asked me back to your place."

She grinned like a fool, tossing some hair over her shoulder. "I can't believe I managed it. Temporary insanity." Or lust.

He circled one hand around her neck and brought her close again, his mouth covering hers and exploring. The kiss was languid, slow, but he drove his tongue deeper, heat building. His body nudged against her as their tongues brushed, sending a thrill of delight through her. When they broke apart again, he was panting. "We should, uh, really finish our dessert. So we can move on to other, you know, things. Like movies we can ignore or character creation."

Giggling like a third grader, she scampered back to her seat. "Oh, yes, of course. That's exactly what I had in mind." A few moments of silence passed as they both devoted themselves to their brownies.

"I knew this table looked familiar."

"I'm... sorry I didn't tell you. I didn't know when would be the right time. But I thought I had a few weeks. I didn't mean to see that text of hers or anything."

"Well, it was a good thing you did. Now if only we can get her to leave us alone."

BY FRIDAY NIGHT, much of the snow had cleared, and the city was moving freely again. Finally he could do things right, like picking her up a few minutes early, the whole enchilada.

In the end, the sushi surpassed expectations. And to his surprise, neither of them heard any more from Ashley. At least not that night. They finished off the night with more peanut butter brownies and coffee, and the night was still young.

When Penny retired to the bathroom for a moment, he went for his bag. The slate-gray carpet of Penny's apartment was surprisingly soft as Nick spread out the player's manual, character sheets, notebooks. She hadn't exactly said she'd play with him, but she seemed determined not to impose. So he was going to have to show her she wasn't.

"What's all this?" she said as she rejoined him. Tonight she had a pale green sleeveless sweater over the usual white button-down, bringing to mind all manner of pistachio desserts and tasting *her* in particular.

He cleared his throat. "Want to make a character for next Wednesday?"

"You mean the night that I'm working while you're playing?"

"The forecast is looking terrible. No one will be there. C'mon. Even if you don't play tomorrow we could make a character for another night."

She stretched out beside him, warm and smelling like a cinnamon roll. "Are you sure I won't be in the way?"

"Definitely."

"All right, how does it work?"

"Well you have to pick a race and a class, to start."

"A race? What kind of game is this?"

"Like dwarf or elf. Like *Lord of the Rings* races. Not real-life ones."

"Oh, okay. Let me see." Penny started paging through the book. "How many are there?"

"Nine races, twelve classes."

"How the heck do you pick?"

"Well, it's a role-playing game. What kind of role do you feel like playing? Here, let's look at classes first." He flipped a few pages forward. "Some of them are more about running around smashing things, some of them are about magic. Some love nature, or stealing and sneaking, or even performing."

"Like singing songs?"

"Yes. Traveling-minstrel style."

"Huh."

"You don't seem to be the loudest trumpet in the band, so I'm guessing not that one. Unless, you know, you want to pretend to be an extrovert for an hour."

She snorted. "Yeah, that sounds exhausting. What do the others play?"

"Good question. Bob is a fighter. I think he's trying to relive his army days—except in a fictional fantasy world I made up for him. Dorothea is a cleric because I think she liked the idea of healing people. Eddie is a warlock. Probably something about the whole serving dark gods thing."

Penny burst out laughing.

"His *character*, not him."

"Is there a difference?"

"Well, yes and no. I mean, obviously you make choices as your character. You get to explore a side of your personality you might not normally get to in real life. But you also can try out acting in ways you normally wouldn't. See if you like it. Experience some other facet of life."

"What do you like to play?"

"Paladin. I sort of dig the whole white-knight thing." Even if maybe he should really be playing a dark knight instead.

"That figures. I should have known. What's this one? Ranger? That lady looks fun."

"Okay, let's do it. She's an elf. Want to stick with that?"

"Well, I mean, I don't identify as a dwarf. Let's try it. Oh— before I forget. My mom has this work get-together next week. Thursday, I think? Her boss is throwing a shindig since it's the tenth anniversary of their firm."

"Wow. And... ?"

"I think he's just throwing to keep them all from going insane during tax season."

"Oh yeah?"

"Yeah, tax accountants regularly work sixty hours plus during tax season." She shuddered. "I'm not looking forward to it."

"Couldn't you do some other kind of accounting? Although... you don't much seem to look forward to any of it."

She shrugged. "We'll see. Anyway, family and friends are invited. Probably so the workers can, you know, actually see their families for some time during these three months."

He snorted and inched closer to her, rubbing her shoulder.

"So you want to come with me?"

He raised an eyebrow. "And meet your mom?"

"Yes. And keep me from losing my mind with boredom. Or being mauled by older, frisky accountants."

"Does that really happen?"

"No. Not at all, really. But I thought it might appeal to your white-knight side."

"It does."

"So you'll come?"

"I wouldn't miss it." He eased his arm around her and squeezed her close for a moment. "Now, about this ranger of yours…"

PENNY'S MOM'S office was one of the grayest places Nick had ever seen. Even the walls wore pinstripes, and the air smelled faintly of cheap, burnt coffee and a vanilla candle the receptionist had set out in a half-hearted attempt to make the area—or her area, at least—feel homey. The lobby also featured a few shamrocks and leprechauns taped to the walls that were the only break in the black-and-white scene. Nick couldn't have been a photographer without having some appreciation for the beauty of black and white, but this was far from the best use of the colors.

A large conference room had been cleared of chairs, its table pushed far to one side, and men and women in suits or high-heeled ensembles milled around, smiling pleasantly, if woodenly. Most of them were coworkers who were probably sick of each other, after all, so it wasn't like Nick was expecting a mosh pit. Beyond a table topped with several bottles of wine, a veggie tray and a cheese platter were the social hubs of the room.

He'd worn one of his wedding getups, khakis and a blue-green button-down, complete with trimmed beard and Nikon around his neck in case it came in handy, but he still wasn't sure if he'd dressed up enough. Now he could see where Penny got her standards. These people knew business formal.

He and Penny had barely acquired glasses of wine, he a

cabernet and she a Riesling, before a well-tailored blond woman was hovering expectantly behind them. Just behind her, a brown-haired version of Penny in a gray dress lurked with a baby on her hip.

"Oh, hey, Mom. Hey, Cass." Penny greeted them both with a hug. "Mom, this is Nick. My boyfriend Nick. And Nick, my mom and my sister, Cassandra."

Nick smiled at her hasty addition of "my boyfriend" as he shook her mother's hand. "Nice to meet you, Mrs. Collins. Cassandra."

"Ms. Collins these days, and yes, it's nice to meet you too." Her smile was warm, though her eyes were a bit tired.

"And I just go by Cass. Or Cassie. And this is Lyle Jr.," said Penny's sister, with a quick switch of the glass to her baby hand to shake. That had to take some skill.

"How are you two enjoying yourselves?" asked Ms. Collins, pouring herself more wine.

"This is a lovely get together," Nick said quickly.

Penny stepped closer, and he slipped his arm around her shoulder and hoped that wasn't overreaching. "We just got here. Everything is very nice. Everyone seems quite tired, though."

"Yep. I bet only half of us will go back to work after this much wine." Penny's mom winked. Nick tried not to let his eyes bug out, as it was well after seven in the evening. "Is that a camera, young man?"

"Yes," Penny hurried to answer. "Nick is a professional photographer."

"Oh, really?" Cass raised an eyebrow. "A photographer of what?"

"Mostly weddings at this point," he said, "but I'm exploring other avenues too."

"Slow time of year then?" said Ms. Collins. "Not like around here."

He nodded. "Has to be slow sometime, I guess. But I do have a client next weekend. Some people like snowy weddings—"

"Can I have your attention please?" A balding man in a black suit stood up on a crate, raising a glass.

"You'll have to excuse me." Penny's mom rushed to refill her glass before the toast.

Penny leaned closer, whispering, "That's my mom's boss. Andrew. He owns the firm. The other partner's kind of retired." Nick tried not to stiffen as Cass eyed them, a not-so-friendly glint in her eyes.

"Thank you all for joining us tonight. I'm so honored to work with you all, to have you here for Leenik & Leonard's tenth anniversary. I always knew we'd make it this far, but I'm proud to see the day has come. Thank you all for coming, and enjoy the wine." He raised his glass.

Nick set down his own, quick as he could, and started snapping. Only after he'd captured a few dozen shots around the room did he retrieve it and clink glasses with Penny. Both she and her sister were staring at him quizzically. He shrugged. "You never know. He might like to have them." He took a swig of wine.

"Maybe if he ever stops working," Penny whispered, grinning.

A few minutes later, Ms. Collins waved Penny and Cass over.

"Want to come? I think I'll get out the cupcakes we brought soon."

He looked down at his nearly empty glass. "I think I'll get a refill. Then I'll join you?"

"Okay."

"Want anything?"

"No, I'm good."

Nick made his way toward the side table where more than a case of wine—or three—had been uncorked and sampled. As he studied the different labels, trying to pick one—if only he knew more about wine—he noticed a woman next to him in casual dress, but the colors were wild. He smelled another creative.

"Looking for something special?" said the woman. She had fiery green eyes, curly red hair, and crow's feet that spoke of many years of laughter.

"Just trying to make sense of the madness." He smiled, picking up another bottle.

86

"Aren't we all? That one's a good bet. With a mild merlot, you can't really go wrong."

"Thanks," he said, pouring some and then offering the bottle to her.

"Don't mind if I do. So what do you do here? One of the accountants?"

"My girlfriend's mother works here."

"Didn't think you fit in. I'm in the same boat. My husband's a CPA." She pointed toward a bunch of folks gathered around Andrew Leenik and clapped him on the back. "So what do you do, then?"

"Photographer." He held up the camera for a moment.

"That how you make sense of the madness, huh?" She smiled as she took a mysterious sip of the wine. Her nails were plain and short, but an emerald glittered on her finger.

"Yes, as a matter of fact." He took his own sip. That was pretty much why the therapist had suggested it, so many years ago. "And you?"

"What do I do?"

"How do you make sense of the madness?"

"I'm lucky enough that for me, those are the same thing. I'm a writer."

"Wow. What do you write?" Nick kept an eye out for Penny as they talked, but he didn't miss Cass watching him, that same, suspicious glint in her eye. They'd barely met—what did she have to be suspicious of?

"I write mostly fantasy, some thrillers. Teen fiction all."

"Sounds great. You are very lucky."

"That's what I tell myself. But I'm making the jump to indie publishing, but I can't find a cover I can stand. Actually, I'm looking for photographers. Do you know anyone that does fantasy photography?"

"No," he said quickly, "but I'd love to give it a shot." He pulled a card out of his shirt pocket to her raised eyebrows. "I'm just getting started, so I'd be happy to give you a good rate. Do you have an email? I can send you some of the weddings and portraits I've done that have a fantasy feel."

"A go-getter. I like it."

Just then Penny waved him over. "Oh, I need to join my girl-friend. Must be time for the cupcakes. Care to join us?"

"No, I'll be trying to drag my husband home soon. Although I suppose I can wait for a cupcake. Are they good?"

"Penny makes the best."

"All right, then," she squinted at the card, "Nick Markov. I'll be in touch. I'm Regina." She held out a hand to shake.

"Great to meet you, Regina. Watch out for that madness."

"I always do."

And he strode back to Penny's side, fingers crossed.

Chapter 8

PENNY'S spare bedroom had been transformed. And not by her paintings on the wall. With her help and blessing, Nick had turned the side of the room opposite the desk into… well, Penny didn't know what she'd call it. But it did make her smile. A long, white sheet of heavy paper hung down from the wall and eased along the carpet, under which he'd laid some boards to make the surface harder. Bright lights shaped like pyramids with the tops cut off stood on each side, aiming wide, luminous bases at the scene.

But what really amused Penny were the models—apparently her mom's coworker's wife had created some characters that looked surprisingly like her friends Vi and Anka.

"Am I doing this right?" Anka muttered, gesturing with the fake bowstaff toward the ceiling. Her back was pressed to Violet's as she made tough faces at the camera, her poker-straight brown hair and lovely large eyes even prettier than normal. In addition to pick-up lines, Anka knew makeup.

"Yes, just like that," Nick muttered from behind the camera. "You're tough. You're strong."

"Oh, I know." Anka gave him a cool, almost haughty look down her nose, and Penny snickered.

"Very good. Think James Bond."

"Or Harry Potter," Penny chimed in. It was fantasy, after all.

"Or Katniss," said Violet, laughing as she pointed her dagger at the camera. The dagger had a day job as a letter opener on Nick's desk.

"Ooh, that wicked grin is perfect. I like it," Nick muttered, and Penny was only a tiny bit jealous none of the characters in Regina's latest series had been blond. Not that she'd have been able to stop blushing anyway.

It turned out Regina had been quite willing to give Nick a chance, especially for Nick's fee of practically nothing. And when Nick had read the character descriptions to Penny to try to figure out how the heck they might find some models, Penny had known just the thing. Er, well, just the people.

"Great work," said Nick, straightening. "Let's try one more thing, and I think we'll have what we need."

"Does anyone need anything to drink?" Penny asked. The lights weren't hot, but the room wasn't getting any colder.

"No, but I'm up for a brownie when we're done."

"Well, then you're in luck, because I have some."

Violet snorted. "When *don't* you have some?"

As Nick rattled off some new pose for them, Penny went to get the brownies out of the fridge and into the warming drawer. Her apartment was feeling less empty every day.

NICK HAD GOTTEN most of his equipment back into the various boxes and cases. Penny's friends had finished their brownies in the kitchen and were packing up to head home themselves when he bumped the mouse of Penny's computer with the corner of his camera bag.

The screen came to life, revealing a gorgeous sunset scene with golds and fuchsias fading into a purple night sky, a tiny dragon soaring amid the layers of gold-rimmed clouds.

He was still standing and staring as Penny came back in.

"They're on their way," she said. "I think they really had fun."

"They did us a big favor, especially since they're getting paid in brownies."

Penny grinned. "Didn't seem to mind." She strode closer and slid an arm around his waist between the bag over his shoulder and his back. "What am I getting paid in?"

"My endless thanks?"

"Try again."

"Sushi?"

"That's a start, but I may have had something else in mind."

He grinned and bent down to kiss her ear. "Oh, I believe *that* is complementary."

"Can I help you down to the car with this stuff? Or do you want to keep it in here in the cold?"

"We can get some out of here now. But hey, before we do—sorry, I bumped your computer accidentally. But this would be perfect for the background of the cover. I could put it in behind them. Can I use it? I'll give you part of the commission."

"The unbelievably paltry commission that was just so there was *some* value at stake? Your words, not mine." She waggled a finger at him.

"Wouldn't it be fun to be paid for your work? Even a paltry amount?"

"You're serious?" Her eyes widened. Almost… afraid?

"Of course."

"That's really sweet, Nick, but…" She was shaking her head.

He squeezed her closer. "Don't make me steal it, Pen."

She snorted and ducked her head.

"It'll take me hours to find and piece together photos to make something half as good as this. If it would even end up that good. Now that I've seen this, I'm going to hate everything I do. C'mon. Save me some time?" He kissed the top of her head.

"Oh, all right. But just don't tell Regina I did it."

"What? Why not?"

"I don't want it to get back to my mom. Or Cass. They don't really know I'm still painting. At least not this much."

"But painting makes you happy, I'm sure they wouldn't—"

"They don't approve. Interferes with schoolwork, you know."

"Yeah, right." He rolled his eyes. "Like your schoolwork challenges you in the slightest."

"You noticed?" It was her turn to squeeze him closer now. "Still."

"They're your family. I'm sure if you talked to them about it—"

"If I talked to them about it, they'd freak."

He waved a hand in the air. "And then they'd eventually get over it."

"No they wouldn't. You don't know them like I do. Especially Cass. She never drops anything."

"Well, that's shitty of them then."

"Nick!"

"What?" He shrugged. "It is."

"They're all I have." She ducked her head again.

"So? That doesn't give them the right to keep your from doing what makes you happy."

Her eyes turned up to meet his, soulful and sad now. "After Dad died, it was hard. Mom had to pick up the pieces. We had totally depended on him."

Oh, they were not getting off *that* easily. "My mom and I have been alone too for a long time. That didn't mean she told me not to go after my dreams."

She sighed. "Look, maybe you're right—"

"Maybe?"

"But they're still all I have. They matter more to me than fighting over these paintings. I'm really okay with that. They mean everything to me. Okay?" She bit her lip, imploring. She wanted him to drop it. Take her word that it was all okay.

The bleakness in her eyes told a different story.

He clenched his teeth and forced a breath through his nostrils. Finally, he sighed. "Okay, Pen. Okay."

THE WINTER WEDDING turned out beautifully, with just a fresh dusting of powder on the ground for the lucky couple's big day. Or so Penny saw from the pictures Nick sent over. She didn't see the wedding, of course, or much of Nick either, as the wedding was promptly followed by a massive bout of the flu.

Can I bring you some soup or something? she texted.

No, my mom's all over it.

He still hadn't shared where he lived yet or invited her over, but he had let slip that it was with his mom—something he hadn't seemed too happy about admitting. While he was covered in germs probably wasn't the best time to meet the parents, anyway.

With all that, it was over a week before Penny could see him again.

Think you'll feel good enough to go to Anka's birthday tonight? I know it's a Tuesday, but...

I'm totally better. Wouldn't miss it.

The wild kiss he'd given her when he'd shown up at her door had her wondering how long they'd actually last at the party. Especially since Anka lived on the second floor of the same building.

"Hey Penny, hey Nick! So glad you guys could make it!" exclaimed Anka as she opened her door.

"Mint brownies—your favorite." Penny held up a tray. "Happy birthday!"

"Aw, thank you! *These* are not going out with the snacks. Help yourself to the wine and cheese over there."

While Anka was one of her best friends, Penny didn't know many of the other folks at the party—or she chose not to. They found a corner to tuck into, and Nick downed red wine while she sipped a little white.

He leaned closer to whisper in her ear. "I missed you."

She stifled a giggle. "Oh, you have no *idea* how much I missed you." She'd actually had to pull her vibrator out of the drawer for the first time in quite a while. It hadn't really done the job. But waking up alone was even worse.

"Really?"

"I think you're going to find out later."

He leaned back, relaxing against the wall.

"You're too far away, come back here."

He laughed, but relented, circling an arm around her waist where she leaned against the wall.

After another glass of wine, she was the one laughing as his hand drifted lower. And lower. And squeezed.

It was probably time to put the brakes on the alcohol. She led him by the hand toward the kichen at the far end of the apartment, depositing their wine glasses in the relatively empty sink. Sitting alone while the other did so would have been unthinkable.

Then she led the way back to the party that was just kicking into high gear, a louder, heavier beat having taken over the music. Just as they were passing the bathroom, he swung her inside, shutting the door behind them. He thrust her against the wall, running his hands through her hair as his body pressed against hers. Hot and hard and ready.

She stifled a delighted giggle. He had to be pretty drunk, she realized as he yanked at her dress, pulling it up over her hips and running his hands over her thighs, then her butt as he murmured in her ear.

"Are those Pikachu underwear?" His voice was breathless as she nodded. "Oh my God, you are the perfect woman."

Her mouth opened to deny it, and he captured her lips with a kiss. Following her underwear with his fingers, he traced the line down to her core. Two fingers thrust into her hot wetness. Withdrawing his fingers, he broke off their kiss and stuck one finger slowly in his mouth, tasting her. She stared, eyes wide following the movement.

What the hell were they doing? What if someone heard them… Oh, what the hell. They were already in here.

She grabbed ahold of his hair, pulling him closer, and whispered in his ear, "Fuck me, Nick."

He did not need further encouragement. He ripped his button and zipper open frantically, pulling out his cock and stroking it as he rubbed the head against her the smooth fabric separating him from her clit, and she stifled a moan.

"We don't have a condom," he muttered in her ear.

"Shit," she whispered. "Let's go upstairs."

"No. I need to taste you. Now."

"What?"

"Lay down on the floor now," he ordered. He reached over and twisted the lock on the door.

Her eyes widened at his tone of voice, her pulse quickening. Oh, hell yes. If this was how he talked and what he did when he was drunk, she would have to get him wined up more often.

Not hesitating, she hurried to lay down on the floor, spreading her legs before him. He knelt down beside her shoulders, one hand still stroking his cock, and buried his face between her legs, upside down this time.

His beard was coarse against her skin, delicious torment. His mouth was intense, the heat swirling and making her close her eyes in sheer, exquisite pleasure. But she forced them back open again, mesmerized by his hand on his cock just above her.

What if she just… She hesitated only for a moment before she reached for it. As her hand brushed his and closed around his length, he moaned into her. She reached up and licked just the tip, and he froze.

She licked again, on the soft underside, then swirled her tongue around. He trembled. He stopped for a moment and inched up, intense eyes boring into her. Smiling mischievously to herself, she reached a little further and took the whole tip into her mouth, then a little more. He groaned, his hips pushing forward of their own accord, surprising her by filling her mouth with his hot length. Oh, hello. That felt good. Warm skin, thick and hard, slid against her tongue. She squirmed and twisted a little closer as he pumped in and out of her for a second.

"Penny," he whispered, still surprised, stifling another groan.

And then he simply lost it. Maybe it was the time apart, the alcohol, or the first time feeling her mouth around him. She didn't care. He abandoned her core to her delight and rotated up closer to her, cradling her neck with his one hand, tangling fingers in her hair. As he held her with one hand and his hips pumped gently against her, she grew even wetter at the slide of his body in and out of her mouth. The gentleness disappeared with each thrust as he lost control. The intensity of it was almost scary, but at the same time, hot as hell. She had no doubt he would stop in the blink of an eye if she said to. If she needed him to.

His raw desire for her was hotter than anything they'd done together yet. *She* had brought that out of him, not just a natural desire for sex, but an all-consuming one, a need so great he struggled to control it. She loved every groan, every tremble. She longed to bring him closer to the edge and watch just what he would do.

She reached up with her other hand, the one not rubbing the base of his cock, and brushed his balls.

A loud moan escaped his lips, and he caught her offending wrist with his hand. He froze for a moment, his eyes wild, and then he captured the other wrist, pinning them over her head and driving his cock into her mouth faster now, with reckless abandon. Not having her hand to throttle his intensity was a little terrifying, but she rolled with it, a thrill shooting from her hands to her breasts down through to her feet. She twisted her legs at the slick need building inside her, growing exponentially at the feeling of his hands around her wrists, pressing her against the cold tile. The edge of tension, the slight bite of a safe sort of fear, whipped her desire into a frenzy nearing his own.

A moment later, his thrust went deeper, and she gagged a little just before the taste of his hot, salty seed hit her. Well, well. So that's what it tasted like? He backed off quickly, one hand taking over for her mouth for much of the job, his seed still shooting in spurts onto her tongue, but with more control. Reflexively, she swallowed, and then she swallowed again, drinking every last bit of him, taking whatever he would give her.

He slowed to a stop, then drew out, reeling back from her to his knees and releasing her. He stared down at her, panting, his expression a mixture of confusion and exhaustion and relief. She grinned up at him, then sat up. He pulled her into his arms, still panting. "Sorry, baby, I should have…" He looked around, still looking unsure of himself, depleted.

The song changed to a different thumping beat, and suddenly she realized there was no way those moans had been quiet enough to escape notice, even over the music of the party. "Let's leave," she whispered. "Go upstairs."

"I didn't do you," he whispered, looking a little irritated with himself.

"We will when we get up there. More room and softer anyway." She winked at him, struggling to her feet. "I think my butt is asleep."

He stared up at her from his knees for a moment, though, as she pulled down her dress and checked her face in the mirror, half expecting a stray drop of him on her cheek. Nothing. He had good aim, apparently.

"You're so fucking beautiful, Penny," he murmured. "And amazing. Have I told you that? I don't deserve you for a second." He threw his arms around her hips, hugging her to him, and she couldn't deny the pleasure that filled her at those words. Almost better than an orgasm. Almost.

"Don't be ridiculous." She ran a hand over his hair. "You're just saying that cause you're drunk." He most certainly deserved her.

He tried to shake his head while also pressing it against her stomach. She smiled. "No."

"C'mon." She pulled him up, grinning to herself, and cautiously cracked the door open, hoping to God they could sneak out of this party unnoticed.

Out in the hall, once she'd shut Anka's front door, she giggled as she ran toward the elevator and hit the button. He ran after her, not letting her get more than a few feet ahead. When the car came, they got inside, and she jammed the close-door button and the nine button like an idiot until it finally closed, probably no faster for her efforts.

He came at her like an avalanche, pinning her to the wall with his kiss, his fingers again finding their way under her dress and delving into her with new determination. His beard scraped raw and fresh against her chin, her lips. She broke away, gasping for breath, and this time let out a moan. Oh God, she was moaning in an elevator now. What if someone was waiting when they got off?

Thankfully, they were lucky. No one was. He barely let go of her long enough to exit, and even as she fumbled with her keys to open the door, his hands groped hungrily at her ass, then shot up to massage her breast. His hips surged against her from behind, sending a whole new thrill through her. No, he couldn't be ready again, not so soon, but—

Spilling into her apartment, they stumbled toward the bedroom, barely getting the door shut and locked. She collapsed onto her bed, relieved to be a little freer now to receive his delightful affections. His hands yanked her panties down and off her, hiking up the dress again, diving with his fingers back into her as he whispered, "Oh God, Penny, you're so wet." Indeed she was a huge sloppy mess at this point. "You're so ready. I'm not yet." He looked pissed at this fact.

"It's not even been five minutes." She laughed, shaking her head at him. She glanced at her end table, wondering... was this the time? A memory of his loss of control back there sent a shiver of anticipation through her, and she twisted, reaching for it.

"I don't think I can—" he started, probably thinking she was reaching for the condoms. He stilled when she pulled the vibrator out of the drawer, eyes wide, but his fingers slid into her again, starting to pump her harder in excitement.

She smiled. "Want to try this?"

He took it from her and stared at it like she'd handed him Excalibur. She stifled another laugh. He was still quite drunk, wasn't he? Yes, they were definitely doing this again. Now she knew why Anka had kept pushing the subject of alcoholic lubrication. Not that she'd have wanted it the first time, but this was fun.

When his eyes turned back to her, they had a hard glint to them that sent another thrill through her. She had a sense that a door had opened when she'd licked his cock, a door to a secret passageway, and it still stood open. Some amount of control he usually employed wasn't in place. The energy pouring off him was electrifying.

"Lie on your stomach," he ordered.

She stared, mesmerized by the change in him. She had always thought him dreamily handsome, adorably geeky, his long frame sexy, and his cute eyes especially hot when they were warm and laughing. But this man was different while also the same—still Nick, but vibrating with power, with life, with a dominion over her that she could trust. That she could lose herself in. It made her weak, helpless at the sight of him.

"Now," he said, his voice dark and quiet.

She enthusiastically complied. His hands gripped her hips and pulled her off the edge of the bed, and she caught herself with her bare feet flat against the soft carpet. He hiked her skirt up farther, and his hands explored her exposed body, running over every curve and crevice, until she was shaking with need.

His left foot nudged hers outward. "Spread out farther for me, Pen."

Her knees trembled at those words, but she did as he asked, her body crying out for more than just a simple caress. He placed his feet just inside hers, effectively holding her spread open for him.

The vibrator buzzed on without warning and slipped inside of her while his fingers slid down to her clit and rubbed in soft circles. She arched her back in delight, her hair whipping against her back.

"I wanna hear if you like it, Penny," he said, his voice rough. "Loudly."

The vibrator slid out and plunged in again, and she grunted.

"I think you can do better than that."

It exited her again, then came back harder, his fingers intensifying, rubbing her harder, and she let her herself moan.

"Do you want to come, Penny?" he whispered. In and out, then again. Again.

"Yes," she moaned between panting breaths.

"I can't hear you."

"Y-yes," she stammered, reaching for the opposite edge of the bed and missing, the sheets twisting in her fists.

"I think you can shout louder than that."

"Oh God, Nick." It sounded like the whole building could hear her, she'd never moaned so loud. Her hands clawed wildly at nothing.

"Keep going. Do you want to come for me, Penny?"

For him. Yes. God, yes, so much so. "Yes!"

"Beg for it," he whispered.

Her eyes widened, and she buried her face in the bed. At that moment, every inch of her wanted to please him. This was clearly something that got him off, this exchange, and it set her alight as well. But what could she possibly say?

"How?" she whispered, face still buried in the sheets.

He was gloriously unfazed by the question. "Say please."

She hesitated. God, was that a bulge in his jeans against her ass cheek?

"And loudly. I'm not letting you come until you do." His hands slowed, the pressure decreasing.

"Please," she whispered, lifting her face above centimeters above the bed.

He rubbed faster, and she gasped. "Louder. Now. You can do this, Penny. I want to know how much you want this. I want to hear how much you want this."

She raised her head again, emboldened a little by his words. "Please, Nick?" She forced her voice louder. "I want this."

His feet nudged her legs farther apart, and she moaned without even trying this time. She could feel her body approaching the edge —would he stop if she hadn't satisfied him? Back off and make her wait?

"Please," she said louder now, smacking at the bed with a flat palm.

"Getting there."

"Please!" It was a shout, a plea, an opening of her soul to admit her truth in the darkness, to acknowledge the depth of the desire she usually hid behind quiet gasps. "Please! God, Nick, make me come."

His fingers quickened, intense and persistent in their pressure, and her knuckles turned white around the sheets, pulling them underneath her, arching her back again as ecstasy loomed. Her legs tried to close, but he held her steady, his knees, too, now holding her open for him, and just the thought of it finally sent her over the edge.

Her cry was nearly a scream as she writhed against the bed, and his body was warm and close behind her, his cock digging into her hip. When the waves of pleasure had abated, the vibrator dropped beside her on the bed. He unzipped his pants and ripped open a condom.

She bit her lip in anticipation, even in her exhaustion pushing her body back toward him, eager to meet him. Without word or warning, he slammed into her to the hilt, the force of him making her catch her breath.

"You okay?" he whispered.

"Much more than okay," she replied.

"You sure?"

She twisted so he could see her face, her smile. Then she lay back on the bed and whispered, "Please fuck me, Nick."

His hands gripped her hips harder than she remembered him ever doing, as he groaned louder than she had. And if she'd thought he'd lost it before, that had been nothing compared to the wild abandon with which he took her now, his body pounding rhythmic and forceful against hers. His feet shifted, freeing hers, moving closer for better leverage. His balls smacked at her clit, and she arched her back now, out of the sheer pleasure of it.

His hands released her hips, and one seized her hair, pulling her back with delightful force. The other cupped her breast as his body lowered over hers, covering her with warmth for a moment. His fingers found her nipple and squeezed, and she cried out, not sure if that was pleasure or pain or something between the two.

He drew back, renewing the force against her core, but one hand stayed in her hair, holding her in place, bringing new wetness to her body. He slowed for a moment, and his belt briefly jingled and then swished off. Why was he—

She caught her breath as the leather circled her throat in the darkness. He held it at her nape, collaring her, firm but not yet painful, and then he was fucking her again, thrusting her in sharp jerks against the leather.

Oh, hell yes. This was everything.

And then, with the other hand, he smacked her ass. Oh, heavens to Betsy, that felt good. They were *definitely* doing this again.

He smacked her again, the sharp sting more pleasure than any kind of pain, and then he grabbed both of her shoulders, thrusting even harder now. God, that felt good too. Solid. Connected. Marked. Owned… And he did own her, he always had, as surely as the day they'd first had sex and she'd written him down in her history books, as sure as she fawned after him all those months without him knowing she existed. She was his, through and through.

And he was hers too. She'd driven him to this point, to this oblivion, and she reveled in his shout, his growl as he exploded in her, his hands clenching her hard.

He hesitated for a long time before he withdrew. "Be right back." The bathroom light clicked on, and the water ran. She scooted onto the bed, ripped off her dress, and crawled under the covers. It was barely a minute before he was back by her side, his arms tight around her, kissing her as though they hadn't yet had the best sex of her life—or any that night—and he still needed her desperately.

Maybe he did.

Chapter 9

WHEN NICK AWOKE in Penny's bed, she was curled against his shoulder and breathing softly and sweetly beside him. He rolled and slid his hand around her waist, and she sighed against his skin. He smiled, blinking the fog of sleep away. He was getting used to waking up next to her. It was heaven.

Or had last night been? A vague memory of intense satisfaction, of complete and utter fulfillment flitted through him, and then flashes of memory. His body instantly responded, even more ready than usual that morning. But in the light of day, his smile faded. Hell.

He stiffened. Oh, God, what had he done?

A memory of pinning Penny down on someone's bathroom floor and coming in her mouth filled him with a shock of both longing and horror. Damn. How had that happened? Had he forced it on her? Had he lost control? And then another flash, the darkest fantasy of Penny spread before him, shouting, begging him to make her come, and him ordering her to—

Fuck.

What had he done? He glanced down at her sleeping form, then around the room. His eyes caught on his belt on the floor, and he swallowed hard.

Too late. It was too late. He'd had one shot at something special and sweet and pure—and just like that, he'd fucked it up. He'd never get the darkness out, would he? He couldn't escape it, now matter how hard he pretended he could.

And now he'd dragged her into it too.

He almost rose to get in the shower. He wanted space, some time to think of a way to apologize. But… no. He'd slipped from her bed a few too many times. She probably wasn't used to waking up to his face yet because of it. And in spite of whatever deviant sex he'd talked her into last night, he was going to put on a brave face and make sure she knew how much he loved her.

Because he did. It was time he said it. He wouldn't, not today, not to associate it with that past night, but soon.

Whatever she'd dealt with last night, he'd make it up to her by being the best damn boyfriend-partner-whatever she could possibly need. He had to be. He couldn't lose her now. He just hoped he hadn't fucked it up already.

He shifted, something hard pressing into his leg. He reached down and discovered a purple vibrator in the bed. Where the hell had that come from? He set it on the end table.

He rolled back onto his side to watch her sleep, her innocent pink lips parted as she breathed. God. He should have known he couldn't keep his darkness away. Ashley had tainted him, and there was no going back. He'd just have to figure out damage control and hope the same wasn't true of her.

Watching her, he remembered now, sliding the vibrator in and out of her wet body. And damn, she'd been wet. Excited. Hot as hell. Was that true, or just the confused hopes of his drunken horny self?

Her eyes fluttered open. "Hey," she whispered.

"Hey," he forced himself to say back, drawing her into his arms so he wouldn't have to meet her gaze with his guilty one. No, no, he should meet this head on. "Last night—"

She pulled away from him, propping herself up on one elbow

and grinning. "Was amazing! I can't believe we had sex in Anka's bathroom."

He snorted. Of everything, that was what was most notable? "How drunk were we?" He forced a smile to match hers.

"Oh, I wasn't hardly at all. You were quite out of it, though." She grinned wider now, eying him.

"What? Why are you looking at me like that?" Was he blushing now? What was she thinking now that she knew his secret, his dark tastes he'd never intended to share?

" 'Cause I guess what they say about sex sucking while you're drunk isn't true for everyone."

He snorted. "Guess not?"

"We are definitely doing that again."

"We are?" Did she really remember what had happened? It couldn't be.

"But I have class in… thirty minutes. Wanna shower and give me a ride?"

He smiled, relieved to dodge any more discussion of last night. Maybe she'd been drunker than she remembered. Maybe if she'd blacked out, he wouldn't have to confess what a weirdo he was. He could only hope.

He hopped out of the bed. "Let's go then!"

PENNY WAS BUSTLING between her first class and her second, going over the upcoming exam topics in her head, when a voice hit her like a sledgehammer from behind.

"Oh, *hey*, Penny!"

Penny froze, stumbling she stopped so quickly. She'd know that voice anywhere. "Ashley…" She tried to force herself to sound happy to see her old friend, but failed. "Oh! Uh, hey. I'm just headed to class…"

"This is so lucky!" Was that enthusiasm in Ashley's voice sincere or sarcastic? "C'mon. This is fate. We are finally going to have that drink. You have time, right?" Ashley grabbed her arm and dragged her through the door of the nearest establishment—a crunchy sort of place. They were headed toward the bar counter before Penny could even blink. "What'll it be?"

"Ash, it's eleven a.m. I do have some time before my next class, but—"

"So mimosas? Or Bloody Marys?"

"I don't need to go to class tipsy. I haven't eaten anything."

She waved down the bartender and ordered two mimosas and a quiche, Penny shaking her head all the while. The man took the order, asked a few questions, convinced Ash to add on a second quiche, and then drifted to leave them in dreaded privacy.

"So. You and Nick, huh?" Ashley grinned.

Penny tried to keep her smile small, but it rebelled and broke out like the sun coming from behind a cloud. "Yeah."

"So tell me everything. How did you two finally hook up? I didn't know you two ever talked back when we lived together."

"We didn't," Penny assured her. "You used to post about him, but we never met."

"Really? Bizarre."

"Uh, yeah. But he started running D&D sessions at the retirement community where I work on Wednesday nights. So we started chatting."

"Oh, yeah, that's like his community service or whatever."

"He has a good heart."

"He's a fucking teddy bear." The mimosas landed before them in tall flutes, and Ash took a quick drink.

"And his uncle is living there."

"Oh, you mean Bob?"

"Yeah."

"You know Bob isn't *really* his uncle, right?"

Penny pursed her lips. "Yes. But isn't that none of your business to tell me?"

Ash sighed, looking down at the bar. "I suppose you're right." She held up her glass as a toast instead. "To really adorable people fucking each other!"

"Ashley!" Penny's cheeks flushed.

"To getting your cherry popped, then?"

Penny slapped a hand over her face, which was on fire now.

"Well, what are we toasting to then?"

"To me and Nick?" Penny raised her glass, eying Ash warily.

She hesitated for only a second before saying, "To you and Nick." She even sort of sounded like she meant it.

Their glasses clinked, and they each took a sip.

"Well, I'm happy for you, Penny." Ashley set down her glass. "But—"

"Sure you are."

"—I mean, you two *are* doing it, right?" Ash leaned forward.

"Why do you care?"

"Good man like that shouldn't go to waste." Ashley smiled and took another drink.

Penny pursed her lips and fidgeted, looking out the window.

"Well, if you're not yet, you chose well when the time comes. He's very talented."

Ugh. "Do we have to talk about your former sex life? Can we just talk about each other? What about you? How have you been?"

Ashley blinked, turning away and hovering over the champagne glass. "I... I've been good. Working on my side hustle and all that."

"Oh yeah? Are you going to try for funding?"

She sighed. "Honestly, my deadlines at work are killing me. It's always crunch time, every damn week. I barely have any time for my own stuff, and I just don't know if I have it in me to do all that slide-deck money-dance bullshit. Especially if my vagina is going to handicap me anyway."

"Dang. That's rough." Penny frowned and held onto her glass a little tighter.

"Yeah." Ash took another sip, shoulders slumping a little.

"Meet anyone new? Anyone exclusive?"

Her friend's lips pursed. "Why does it need to be exclusive?"

"It doesn't! I was just wondering if anyone had gotten serious."

She shook her head, not meeting Penny's gaze. "Nah. I don't think I'm ever going to find someone." She sat her glass down on the bar. "Some guys are really into their careers, and I don't want to get in too deep if it's just not going to work out with us both being career-driven. Then there's more flexible guys, guys who aren't so driven, but that alone can be a turnoff. And then even when I dig them, it doesn't mean we always share the same... you know, tastes and proclivities."

"Tastes and proclivities?" Penny asked slowly.

Ash side-eyed her. Suddenly Penny felt like she had walked into a trap. "I have some very particular tastes when it comes to sex. If you hadn't figured that out yet."

Penny shrugged, looking back into the drink and mostly not wanting to know.

"As does Nick," Ash said, an edge to her voice.

This was what she'd wanted to get at all along, wasn't it? In spite of herself, a smile broke out on Penny's face. It grew into a giddy grin as she thought of last night's encounter. If *those* were his tastes and proclivities, Penny was all for it, and perhaps they were an even luckier match than she'd realized.

Please, sir, may I have another!

She faked a shrug and said sweetly, "I have no idea what you could mean."

"I'm kind of a twisted fuck, is what I mean. If you ask me. You have a backbone in bed, and it can spin a guy's head around. Some of them like it, some don't. Nick was a rare one who got it. Probably why we kept going so long."

Penny winced. It wasn't fun to think of Nick with anyone else, let alone him having a good thing with them. For a long time. Even if it had been "twisted." Even if he'd broken it off for her. "I don't think this is any of your or my business. You should leave this to Nick. And besides, this is supposed to mean what to me?"

"I mean," Ashley said, "he likes girls, you know, taking the reins, so to speak. Being a little aggressive."

Penny almost spit out her orange juice and spent the next several moments coughing, which conveniently hid the laughter that had boiled out of her at the thought. *That* was what she thought Nick liked? Perhaps he did, but drunken Nick had seemed anything but submissive.

"Look, I just... I wanted to warn you, 'cause that doesn't seem like it would be your thing. I know it's not my business, but I've been in more than one awkward relationship that went south when such tastes didn't match up. That's all." Ashley patted her back as Penny tried to get the last bits of orange juice and champagne out of her airway.

"But it's your thing?" Penny finally choked out.

Ash sighed. "Yeah. I mean, that's what I mean. Hard to find guys for girls like me."

Recovered, Penny took a deep breath. "I'm sure you'll find someone perfect. It's a matter of time," Penny said, enjoying the opportunity to dodge the topic. She doubted Ashley would actually let it slide.

"If you want any pointers or something…" Ashley gave her a helpless shrug that almost seemed truly sincere. Probably a trick, but maybe…

"No, no. I'm good." The silly grin returned. She was so, so good. She would definitely have to broach this topic with Nick— surely Penny could find some way to give as good as she got if he truly enjoyed that—but she had a feeling Ashley was just off her rocker. She didn't seem to have a clue about Nick's true tastes. Penny had seen firsthand something entirely different.

Hmm, could she get him to tie her up? She tucked that thought away for later.

"Well, you know… when you get there or whatever… I'm here to talk, or if you have questions or anything." Ashley downed the rest of her drink. Was she really trying to be helpful? "I could—"

"I don't want to know about any of that. But what I do want to know is, did you ever have any feelings for Nick? I mean, really. I won't tell him."

Ashley met her eye and hesitated, gauging something. "I mean, there are feelings. Gratitude. Affection, respect. Appreciation. I'd like him to be happy. And fulfilled. But love is what you mean, isn't it?"

Penny nodded.

"Then no. I wanted to, I really did. But no. You? How long have you guys been dating anyway?"

Oh, Penny loved him. She didn't know when exactly it had started but… there was no mistaking it now. But she wasn't fool enough to tell that to Ashley before she'd told Nick. "I hope you can find somebody you love, Ash," Penny dodged.

"Me too, but——"

"Oh, hell, no," came a voice from behind them.

Penny spun on the stool to see Nick standing behind them, shocked. No, pissed. His jaw was twitching, and he had that dark look again. Ashley, too, twisted on her stool, leaning her elbows on the bar and relaxing languidly against it. Penny did not miss the way the posture left her knees splayed in Nick's direction, something about it saying, this is still available, you know.

And to Penny's chagrin, his eyes were entirely trained on Ashley, so maybe it was working.

"Hey, Nick," said Ashley, smiling.

"Fuck off, Ash." His eyes turned to Penny now, to her relief, and softened. "Hey, Pen."

She grinned and waved at him.

"I asked you to leave us alone," he said, eyes back on his ex now.

Ash pouted. "What, I can't catch up with an old friend just because you start fucking her?"

He glared daggers at her. "Are you two done 'catching up'?" he asked, his voice hard as stone.

"We sure are." Penny hopped off the barstool and stepped toward him. He slipped his arm around her waist and pulled her against him, a little roughly, but like this spot was the most natural place for her in the world. The aggressiveness of the gesture brought the heat of last night flushing back to her cheeks. Penny tried to ignore Ashley frowning at them. "See you later, okay, Ash?" She risked a glance over her shoulder as they started to walk away.

"Wait——Penny——"

Penny turned back. "Yes?"

Ash had risen. "I… I really am happy for you. I mean that," she said, ignoring Nick now.

Penny paused, then swept back and pulled Ashley into a hug.

"And I meant what I said, you'll find someone," Penny whispered into her ear. "The right someone."

Nodding, Ashley swiveled away. Penny took Nick's hand, and they walked out, Nick glaring over his shoulder all the while.

THERE WAS no reason to freak out. No reason at all. Penny was the same chipper woman as ever, bouncing by his side and swinging his hand back and forth between them like she might start skipping. She glowed in the late morning light. Happy. Content, even.

There was no reason to worry that what had happened last night or her conversation with Ashley had tainted him in her eyes forever.

Repeating it over and over didn't seem to be helping him believe it.

"How was class?" he said instead.

"Fine," she said on a sigh. "I'll be glad to have it done with. This next one should be slightly more interesting, though. I wish I could get into it like Anka can. What are you doing so close to campus, by the way?"

"Met with a professor about her wedding coming up in May. Gotta start lining them up early. It was supposed to be coffee in Hendricksberg, but she asked if I could meet her here at the last minute, and since I had just dropped you off…" He shrugged.

She squeezed his hand.

Were they *really* not going to talk about the elephant in the room?

"Pen, I…" How to broach this delicate subject?… Penny, did my ex-girlfriend tell you all the deviant things I did with her that I'm kind of ashamed of but also thought were massively hot? At least some of them? Yes, you know, like the ones I did to you last night except I don't entirely remember…

"So… how did things end with you two again?" she said before he could go further.

He raised an eyebrow. "I broke it off with her. Three months ago."

"Ah." She grew quiet for a moment, eyes on her toes. "Did you ever wish you two were exclusive?"

He frowned. This certainly wasn't what he had expected. "At first I did. But to be honest with you, I was just happy to be getting any." He sighed at his former, foolish self. "Kinda stupid. Sophomore me had a few more... insecurities." And had still been kind of shocked any girl wanted him. "On the other hand, I pretty much *was* exclusive. I went on a few dates but not much more than that. But wishing we were exclusive... that may have been more like jealousy than actual caring. Or competitiveness. She was always scoring more points. After a while, I kinda stopped caring. Maybe the sting wore off. Or maybe I just quit paying attention to it."

"And so in the end you just got bored? Quit texting?"

He laughed. "If only." She wanted more details about this? That couldn't be good. "You know Ash. I had tried that before, and it hadn't worked. It was more I told her it was over, I wasn't going to see her anymore. She burned some of my stuff."

"Ouch. So it was your choice?"

"My choice. Penny, why are you asking about this?" He stopped, gripping her arm. "Was it something she said?"

"Nothing she said. I can tell she still wants you, that's all." She looked all around the street before meeting his eyes.

"Oh." He hadn't really been paying much attention. Ash wanted everybody, it seemed. Didn't she? But he had secretly suspected her conversation with Penny might have been designed to break them up and get him back. He'd just been hoping that was wildly self-centered of him. Perhaps not.

"You've been visiting Bob at the center for, what, four months?" Penny said.

A smile stole into his face. "Heh. Yep."

"You broke it off because of me?"

"Well, I should have really done it *long* before that. But you were the catalyst that made me actually bother to deal with the bullshit." He squeezed her arm.

She stepped closer and slipped her arms around his waist,

resting her head against his shoulder for a moment. Then she looked up and smiled. "Let's keep going."

"What did Ashley say?" He forced out the words.

"Oh, a few things." Penny studied the pavement and waved it off as if it was all of no great importance. Hopefully she was right. She was smiling now, at least. "She offered her congratulations. Tried to pump me for details. Wanted to know if I'd sacrificed my virginity on your altar yet."

"Your choice of words or hers?"

She grinned. "Mine. But I don't think about it like that. Just... role-playing I guess?"

If he hadn't already been sure he loved her, that moment might have done it. "Well, you can make a sacrifice at my altar anytime." He winked.

"Look, I have to get to this last class, and then I've got tons of studying for my exam on Thursday. And my sister is stopping over later. So we may have to wait till the weekend or something..."

"How about after your exam?" He grinned. "After I get off work Thursday. Pretty please?"

"Oh, all right. I'll text you?" Her bright smile, even as a cold wind whipped around them, eased him a little. Even if his logical mind thought it didn't make any sense.

He leaned down and gave her a quick kiss. "Have a good class, Pen. Later."

And she walked off, arms swinging like she didn't have a care in the world. Hopefully, she was right.

Chapter 10

PENNY GROANED and shoved the textbook aside. Another minute of studying, and she was going to go insane. The exam was tomorrow morning. She had gone over everything in triplicate. Maybe it would be enough for now... Or maybe she'd just take a short break and get back at it again.

Her mind drifted back to Anka's party—or more specifically its aftermath. Tomorrow she'd have time to see Nick again, and perhaps they could revisit some of those... activities. Nick hadn't seemed quite himself afterward, though. A little stunned and freaked out. How could she show him she'd enjoyed the encounter as much—if not more than—he had?

She wandered into her bedroom and pushed around a few boxes like a bad Tetris game. There. Halloween decorations—and costumes.

Zipping off the packing tape, she dug to the bottom of the box, looking for a costume Ash had talked her into freshman year. Sexy policewoman. It sure had had the boys drooling then. And Penny blushing and Ashley laughing at her pink cheeks.

Not her fondest college memories. But that wasn't the point. There—found them! Handcuffs! Nice ones too, Ash had commented, not the usual cheap costume kind. That had been more of an accident than intentional, as Penny had ordered them online a little hastily.

Perhaps it had been fate.

She shook her head now, thinking of Ash's reactions. She should have guessed her friend's "tastes and proclivities" sooner.

Closing up the box, she sat the cuffs on the dresser. That'd be a surprise for Nick—one that might push him in the right direction.

She shuffled back out into the living room and flopped down on the couch. Her study break needed to be at least a *little* longer. Her eye caught on the quarter she'd been using to play around with the *I Ching* for next week's club meeting. What was better for a study break than a little meditation… or meditative fortune-telling?

She picked up the cold, smooth disc of the quarter. She needed a question.

How about… what lay in store for her and Nick? Tell me the future, little coin.

Six tosses, six lines recorded on her little notepad, and she had a hexagram to punch into the app on her phone that included the sixty-four hexagram library. Hexagram thirty-one…

Hexagram thirty-one was called *Wooing*. She snorted at the phone, *Mutual Attraction*. Well, that was apt. *The joyful lake meets the stable energy of mountain*, she read. *The masculine takes the initiative, then submits to the feminine. The lake's water nourishes the mountain, while the mountain causes the rain to fall. Thus is the balance of heaven and earth, the dance of courtship, two more complete when together than without.*

Well, she couldn't argue with that. Nice to get a happy outcome once in a while.

A knock on the door broke through her thoughts.

"Cass!" she called. "You're early."

Her sister greeted her with a half-hearted smile. "Sorry. Lyle came home early for once, since he knew I was coming over here, and I just had to get out. Ready for some 'me' time?"

"If you can call baking that."

"I do! When it's with you."

"Then absolutely."

. . .

NICK WAVED goodbye to Carl as he zipped up his black pea coat. "Have a good rest of the night, Carl!"

"You too, Nick. Enjoy your Thursday."

The icy air hit him like a bucket of water as he stepped outside, and he dug into his pocket for his keys, rushing to get to the car just as someone stepped in front of him.

"You stay away from my sister."

Nick stopped short, looking up from the coat to see none other than Cass. He could only stare for a long moment. "Excuse me?"

"You heard me. I want you to leave Penny alone."

"I care about Penny. What's this about, Cass?"

"You care about her? Oh really? I'm her family. I've been looking out for her a lot longer than you have. And I want you to stay away from her."

"No way—"

"Penny needs someone that can provide for her. Not some two-bit kid with a photography hobby and a part-time job."

He covered his shock with a cough. "Isn't that up to her to decide? Maybe you should stop pushing her around and meddling in her life. She can take care of herself."

"Oh really? Is that what these are for then? Letting her take care of herself?" Silver flashed as Cassie pulled something from her pocket—handcuffs.

Nick's blood went cold. "What—where did you get those?"

"Penny's. I found them when I stopped over yesterday. Blatantly sitting on her *dresser*, no less."

He'd never… had he somehow left them there that night after Anka's party? But he would never have—he couldn't have— He groped for something to say to defend himself, but came up with nothing. Exclaiming they couldn't possibly be his didn't seem like that'd convince anyone.

"It seems to me like *you're* the one pushing her around, if this is any indication. My sister would never have had these before you came around. I'm telling you—stay away from my sister, you sick, twisted fuck."

For a moment, he could only stare, blinking. Then the situation fell on him with its real weight, like a wrecking ball to the skull. He'd tried to push the darkness down, he'd tried to hide it, but his secret had escaped anyway. In a way worse than he'd ever imagined.

"But I can't just disappear," he started. "Penny will wonder—"

"You can, or I'll tell this whole town about your dirty little hobby. Is it because she looks so young and innocent? Or just that she does what she's told?"

"What? Jesus, it's none of that. Just wait a minute, Cass, I *love* Penny, I'm not—"

"You will, or you'll never work in this town again."

NICK DROVE home in a zombie-like trance, each turn a fresh cut of pain. He should have been on his way to Penny's by now. He should be there by now.

Nick sank down on his bed and looked for a way out. Anything. Nothing came to him.

If it had been just the handcuffs… maybe he could have talked to Penny about it. They needed to talk about it anyway, much as he'd been putting it off. And he doubted Cass could tell that many people his secret, if she'd even follow through on the threat. Mortifying as hell, but he'd probably survive. Maybe move to another town, worst-case scenario.

But it wasn't just the mysterious handcuffs. Not really.

Penny had already made it clear that she would listen to her family on most things. Important things. Painful things. He couldn't imagine his mother telling him to give up photography, but if she did… Well, he couldn't imagine listening. But Penny wouldn't move to follow him if Cass ruined Nick's career here.

Maybe Penny just loved her family more than he did. As if she would choose him over her family? Fat chance. And he didn't *want* to make her choose. That'd be an asshole move if he'd ever heard of one. Not that it had been his idea.

Fucking Cass.

But the truth was… Penny would abide by their wishes. She had before, and she'd do it again. And therefore, so would he.

Sorry, can't make it tonight.

He typed the text and sent it as quickly as he could, like ripping off a Band-Aid. If doing so tore open a horrible, gaping wound.

The text didn't make any sense. She'd have to wonder what was going on. But that was inevitable, because his breaking things off didn't make any sense. If he just didn't show up, she'd think something had happened until she finally got in touch with him, so at least the text would minimize that confusion.

He threw the phone on his desk in disgust and went upstairs to look for some gin. All he found was light beer and cheap rum.

It would have to do.

Fucking Cass. How dare she. And how dare she be *right*. This was better for Penny anyway.

She deserved to be free to go find herself some cashmere-turtle-neck-wearing supermodel cardiothoracic surgeon who had made more of himself than getting really good at a low-paying hobby.

And Nick… well, Nick would be free to get really fucking drunk. And to know that for at least a few weeks, he'd known heaven.

Chapter 11

PENNY TRIED for the third time to get the curve of the wing on the green dragon right. Nearly everything about him had come together, but for some reason this one wing just hated her. She eased the stylus along the digital tablet, drawing it into the computer for the dozenth time. Hmm, closer, but still no cigar. She made a new layer and tried again, screwing up her nose at the obstinate creature.

This was way better than that stupid exam. Just a few more, plus the CPA exam, and she'd be free of this nonsense. Well, not exactly. She'd be free of tests—but then have to pursue some path full-time. Nothing was certain but death and taxes—doubly so for her. The thought slumped her shoulders. Hmm, where was that chocolate she'd left somewhere around here?

At least in her spare time she could play with dragons like these. And she had someone supportive like Nick to appreciate them. She straightened up in her seat and made another go at the wing.

A few minutes later, her phone vibrated on the desk beside her.

Sorry, can't make it tonight.

Penny stared down at the text. It didn't even sound like something Nick would write. Had somebody stolen his phone? What the hell?

What is it? she wrote back. *Something wrong?*

But even as she asked it, she knew, deep down, that something was very wrong. She just didn't know what.

More than a quarter of an hour passed, but no response came.

She pushed the stylus and the tablet away as her gut churned. It didn't make any sense. He'd never canceled anything with her before, let alone at the last minute. She tried texting again.

Did something happen? Just worried. Was it something I said? Feeling ok?

Nothing.

About halfway through the lonely, unnaturally long evening, she started texting Anka, but her friend had no more answers than she did.

Penny tried one more time at bedtime. Then again the next morning, despite the black hole yawning wide in her gut that something was seriously, seriously wrong.

Good morning, handsome. Miss you.

The text eventually was marked as read, but no response came.

Her heart just about cracked in two.

BY SUNDAY, Penny was a red-eyed, snotty, anxious mess. While she and Cass had baked a full batch of cupcakes on Wednesday for that weekend's community bake sale in Cass's cul-de-sac, Penny had tried a bit of baking therapy. She'd had too many unwanted hours suddenly free on the weekend—and now she had two dozen brownies and a score of rice crispy treats to donate to the sale as well.

Which was good, because if she ate them all, no amount of walking around her neighborhood would burn that much off.

She also couldn't stand her dreadful, silent, empty apartment anymore. It was too much a ghost, a shell of what had been.

He was everywhere.

Mittens and boots deposited in the elegant, high-ceilinged foyer, Penny unwound her pale gray scarf as she dropped into one of Cass's delicate white kitchen chairs.

"I just don't know what could have happened." The words

bubbled out of her, almost before she intended to say anything. Or bring up the subject. "Wait—where's Lyle Jr.?"

"He's napping." Cass set the brownies on the counter with a smile. "For once."

"Oh, that's good." She shrugged out of her coat now as well. "But you've gotta understand. He's never done this before. I don't understand it. Anka doesn't either, or Violet. But he won't respond to my texts and explain! Does this mean we're breaking up?"

"What a jerk." Cass scowled as she drifted over to settle in the chair across from Penny. "To just drop you like that. Do you want some tea? Would that help?"

"Sure. But Cass, he's not a jerk. He's one of the kindest men I know. I can't understand it. It's not like him."

Her sister rose and hit the button on the electric teapot beside her plant-adorned kitchen window. "Look, sis, I know he means a lot to you, being your first major boyfriend and all. But there'll be others."

"Others?" Penny blinked. "I don't want others. I want him."

"I dated a lot of guys before I met Lyle. I know the first one always seems really great. Like you'll never get over them or find anyone better. But then you do. You will." She shrugged as she returned to sit at the table while the kettle worked its magic. "The pain goes away eventually."

"It's only been a few days, Cass. I don't want your advice on how to get over him, I want your advice on how to get him back. Or at least to respond to my texts."

"I thought you came to visit and drop off baked goods."

"Only because I'm in a state of emotional catastrophe."

Cass grimaced. "Who says you need him back?"

"I do." Penny set her jaw, eyes fixed on the table. There *had* to be something she could do. There just had to be.

"I just mean, maybe you're better off without him."

"What the hell do you mean?"

"He's still young, still struggling in his career—"

"So? Who isn't, at my age?"

"Lots of people. Besides, why limit yourself to people your age?"

"Cass, why are you trying to talk me out of this? I don't want out of this."

"Next week, with a little distance from him, you might not feel so bad."

Penny groaned. "You are no help at all."

Cass pressed her lips together. "Frankly, Penny, he seems pretty determined to pursue a career that will never pay off. Don't you think that's a little juvenile? Irresponsible? Selfish even? If you're really thinking about this man for the long term, are you sure you want to shackle yourself to someone who can't hold up their end of the family bargain? He'll never be able to provide for you."

"I didn't realize you're an expert on professional photography markets now."

"You'll always be supporting *him*. Is that what you want?"

"I don't need to go your path, Cass. I don't need someone to provide for me." Or want it, either.

"Money doesn't grow on—"

Penny smacked a palm on the table. "Damn it, I know that. That's why I am getting this stupid degree in the first place."

"It's not stupid, it'll provide you with a stable, reliable income."

"If that's so important, why did *you* quit your job, then?"

Cass stopped cold at that, her eyes darkening.

"And what does any of this have to do with Nick not responding to my texts? Are you seriously suggesting I should break up with the man that I love over how much money he makes?"

"Love?" Cass's eyes went wide. "Don't you think that's taking it a little far?"

"No, actually, I don't think it's taking it too far. And I would never break up with someone because of how much they make."

"Well, I'm sorry, honey, but it seems like he's breaking up with you."

Penny gasped, sitting back for a moment, her hand on her chest. Just then the tea kettle hit its boil, a light flashing as hot steam erupted into the kitchen air. Cass rose to make the tea.

"I *know*," Penny whispered almost to herself as the water burbled noisily into two mugs. "But what I want to know is why."

"Does it matter? Men are fickle." Cass flicked her fingers at the air with one hand as the other set down the kettle on its base.

"Nick's not."

"They all are. I was just trying to point out the silver lining of the situation."

"Even Lyle? By the way, where is he?"

"Working overtime again."

"At two p.m. on a Sunday afternoon?"

"That's the definition of overtime, I think." Cass's eyes were dark, hung up on the mug she sat in front of Penny and then gliding bleakly to her own.

"Wow, that's—"

"I don't want to talk about it."

"Is there something going on?

Cass took a deep, ragged breath. "To be honest with you, I'm a little worried he's cheating on me. It isn't just the working late. There were some charges in our bank account that don't make any sense. One was for flowers. And when he comes home, he's distant."

Penny sat back in the chair, floored. "My God. Did you talk to him about it?"

"No. What can I say? I can't say anything. I'm just dowdy and unshowered all the time. I've gained five pounds. I'm nowhere near losing the baby weight. I can't even remember where my lipstick is, let alone the last time I put it on. Who can blame him?"

"What? Don't think like that. Cass, that's awful. And none of that is true. You look better than ever."

"Yeah, right."

"Maybe you just need some time off together. A date. A getaway. I can watch the little one."

"No. You have school—"

"Look, school doesn't take up one hundred percent of my time. Especially if I'm gonna have so much more free time without Nick around. You still care about Lyle, don't you? More than that, you love him? Right?"

At that, Penny was surprised to see tears rim the edge of Cassie's eyes. "Of course I do."

"Well then, you've got to do whatever it takes to get him back. Just like I'm going to do whatever it takes to get Nick back. Just as soon as I can figure out how."

"Penny…" Cass was wringing her hands now, not looking at all relieved.

"What? What is it?"

"Don't do that." The tears hadn't left Cass's eyes.

Penny stared for a moment, trying to understand. "Do what? Babysit for you? It's the least I can do."

"No. Don't try to get Nick back."

"Why?"

"I just don't think you're good for each other. You'll be better off without him."

"How can you say that? I love him, Cass." Had loved him for years at a distance, although Cass didn't know that. And he was so much better than she'd imagined. Sir Dreamy seemed like a distant, foggy, well, dream when compared to the real man in high definition. "I'm not giving up this easily."

"Penny, I… it's not just the money thing, the career thing." Cass frowned, looking down in her lap. "Look, I know I shouldn't have been snooping around, but I wasn't trying to, really. But when I was at your place the other day, I found these."

Penny froze and stared as Cass set the pair of silver handcuffs on the table. The ones Penny had set on the dresser, hoping to show Nick the next day. That she'd forgotten to put away or hide when her *sister* was coming over.

Penny swallowed. "So?"

"What do you mean, so? So if he's making you do things you don't want to do—"

"He's absolutely not. What would even make you think that?"

"What are these for then?"

Penny shrugged, trying to play it casual. "Role-playing. Fun. What else?"

"Do you mean you're *okay* with this?"

"Okay with what?"

"With this kind of deviant behavior? What kind of guy gets off on tying girls up, Penny? Doesn't that scare you?"

"No." When had Cass become such a prude?

"Come on! Everyone knows this kind of shit is sick. This is probably a sign he was abused. Or has watched *way* too much porn."

"Those are both myths. Consensual role-playing and power exchange can be perfectly healthy and very fulfilling." That came out surprisingly confident, considering she'd only read it online a few times now. She still had a lot more research to do. She was *totally* not prepared for this conversation. And what did it matter if Nick never talked to her or touched her ever again?

"Consensual role-playing? What? I can't believe what I'm hearing!"

"Cass…" Penny reached out and closed her hand around the cuffs. "These aren't Nick's. They're mine."

Cass stared, mouth hanging open. "What?"

"They're mine."

"*Yours?* Penny—my God. You must stay away from this man. A few weeks of having sex and you're into S&M?"

"Technically, this is only very light bondage."

"What will a year bring, public orgies?"

"No, it won't. Jeez, get a grip."

Cass's eyes hardened, glinting in the silvery tones of her kitchen skylights. "This is way out of control. I am *so* glad I told him to stay away from you."

Penny's blood ran cold. "Excuse me? You what?"

Cass straightened, her chin rising in that stubborn way that used to make Penny want to punch her. Wait—scratch that. It *still* made Penny want to punch her. "I told him to stay away from you. And I don't regret it."

"How could you do such a thing?" Penny cried.

"Anyone who gets off on this kind of thing is fucked-up and not someone that is right for you. My little sister deserves better. *You* deserve better. Someone kind, someone that can support you—"

Penny stabbed a finger at the table. "For your information, Nick Markov is the kindest, most considerate man I have ever met. Lyle could take a few lessons from him. Nick's never *made* me do anything I don't want to do, and he's not fucked-up."

"Oh, what are you, a psychologist now?"

"I'm not, but neither are you. Listen to me. How I choose to have sex and with whom is up to me and me alone. Do you hear me? *Not* you." Penny wasn't sure when it had happened, but she'd risen to her feet and was pounding on the table. She sank hastily back down. "Just what did you tell him?"

"I told him you deserve someone who could better provide for you."

Penny winced.

"And I told him that I knew about his sick little fetish, and that I'd tell everyone in town about it if he didn't stay away from you."

Something in Penny hardened from horror to rage to cool, righteous anger now. "Well. That explains a lot. I guess I came to the right place to figure out what happened with Nick."

"Penny, I'm just trying to look out for you. This is for the best."

"Well, stop. I've had enough of your 'looking out for me.' It was one thing to stop painting. It was one thing to focus on my schoolwork and give art up for now. To relegate my passion to a hobby. But you're not going to pressure me into giving up Nick. And I'm starting to realize I should've never let you pressure me into *any* of it."

Penny snatched the cuffs off the table and stormed toward the door, jerking on her coat.

"Penny, wait—where are you going?"

"To find Nick and make this right."

"Wait. Let's talk about this." Cass rushed after her as she slammed her feet into her boots. Couldn't happen fast enough. "You could have anyone, sweetie. Anyone!"

Penny yanked the door open and stopped to look back at her sister for a moment. "I don't want *anyone*, I want him. You're not going to change that. Maybe you should quit meddling in my business and start worrying more about your own. You must have married Lyle for a few things other than his money and his good looks. Maybe you should be remembering what they are."

Penny slammed the door behind her and stomped out toward the street. It was a low blow, but she couldn't bring herself to care.

HUDDLING outside at the nearest bus stop, Penny jammed Ashley's number into her phone. A bleary voice answered, slurring, "What?"

"Give me Nick's address," Penny demanded.

"What?" At least she sounded awake now.

"Nick's address. You have it, right?"

"Wow, what's going on? Little Miss Perfect finally coming to me for some sex help?"

"No, I'm coming to you for Nick's address. Do you have it or not?"

"Hold on, I need to wallow in this feeling for a moment."

"I'm hanging up." Penny lowered the phone.

"Wait! Wait, I have it."

She raised the phone to her ear again.

"Where are you? Are you going over there?"

"Yes."

"When?"

"Right now."

"Jesus, some shit really hit the fan. What happened?"

"I don't want to talk about it. I just need to get over there and see him."

"Okay, hold on, I'm finding it. But listen, his mom is nosy as hell. You're going to need more than just the address." On the other end of the phone, something rustled, then clanged. A cabinet shutting.

"What are you doing? I swear, if you're just jerking me around—"

"I'm *not*. I'm coming to get you. Where are you?"

"What?"

"Where are you? The buses don't run often out Nick's way. I'll come pick you up."

Penny sat stock still, the hard anger in her heart at her sister easing a little. Was Ash for real? "I'm at my sister's. Well, the bus stop outside. On Yardvale Street and Dixon."

"Got it. Be there in a few." Ashley hung up.

Penny stared down at the phone. If this was some sort of trick, Penny was going to *kill* her.

But sure enough, about five minutes later, Ashley pulled up in her black hatchback and motioned for Penny to get in. Sitting on the seat was a DVD.

"My copy of *While You Were Sleeping*? Damn it, Ash, you said you lost it."

Ashley shrugged in her leather jacket. "Well, I found it."

"Where are we going?"

"To Nick's. I texted you the address. But first we need to make a quick stop at the drive-thru."

"Ash," Penny started, barely concealing the pain in her voice, "this is no time for a snack while I'm freaking out over here——"

"It's not for me. It's for you. His mom is a sucker for rom coms and fried chicken. So you can have some time without interruptions for the state that you're in."

"What state am I in?"

"Seems like half past bust-down-his-door and a quarter to knock-some-sense-into-him, if you ask me. Which you did. What happened?"

"I don't know. That's what I'm going there to find out."

Chapter 12

NICK OPENED HIS EYES, no idea what time it was. His desk lamp cast a tiny amount of illumination in the dark room. It could have been midnight. It could have been noon. He was in a dungeon of his own making—and not the fun kind. No, not ever again. Darkness had stolen happiness from him, and now he didn't think he'd ever get out.

How long had he been in bed? How long had he been asleep? It didn't matter.

What had woken him up? A more interesting question.

The door to his basement abode creaked open. "Nick!" Mom called.

"What." He barely made the effort for her to hear him.

"Uh, your girlfriend—and your ex-girlfriend?—are here to see you."

He lurched upright, glancing around in panic. Bottles were scattered across the dresser. Where was his shirt? His usually tousled hair was outdoing itself. He hadn't bathed. Or brushed his teeth. Or —what the hell was Penny doing here? And did that mean she was with Ashley?

Maybe they were here to kill him. Or at least beat him senseless for senseless cruelty.

It only seemed fair.

But only one set of soft footsteps made their way down the stairs. Penny appeared at the bottom, shucking her coat and sky blue scarf at the foot of his bed as he hauled himself to a seat at the edge. The world lurched. He couldn't have been asleep *that* long, because he was still somewhat drunk. He ran a hand through his hair. No, stop it, that's probably only making it worse.

"This isn't exactly how I imagined you seeing my room." He peered up at her warily.

"Nick. You look like hell." Her frowning eyes skimmed across his face. His bare chest. He could feel attraction crackle between them. He wanted to pop the buttons on that white dress shirt of hers and bury his face in pale lace.

But he couldn't. Never again. "I'll bet," he grumbled instead.

"What the heck is going on?"

"I…" How could he explain? Did he explain what happened? Somehow he didn't think Cass would want Penny to know. He swallowed. No, he should probably play along. Finish the job. Let her go. Like a man. Shut up and handle the pain. Let her go on to greener pastures. "You shouldn't be here, Penny," he said softly.

"Why not?" She strode over to him, stopping just short of him and propping her hands on her hips. He looked up at her, like a kid in trouble with his teacher. She even had the wardrobe for the part.

He swallowed, searching for words as he gazed up into her frowning blue eyes, but he found nothing. The alcoholic haze wasn't helping. He could smell her, all sweetness and baked goods. The image of her on her bed limned by the moon sprung back to his mind, twisting the knife.

"Why aren't you answering my calls? My texts?"

He shook his head. What could he say to that?

"Damn it, what happened?"

"I can't talk about it," he finally mustered. She bent down, bringing her face close to his, angelic and intoxicating. "I can't… God, you're so… Oh, Penny."

He wanted to pull her close, press his cheek to her stomach, breathe her in. He hung his head in his hands.

She frowned harder. "How much have you had to drink?"

"I never deserved you."

Her voice sharpened. "How much have you had to drink?"

"How many bottles are on the desk?"

"Nick! That's ridiculous."

"It's taken most of the weekend, if it makes you feel any better."

"Have you had any water?"

"What? No."

She grabbed a nearby glass of clear liquid. "Here, drink this."

"That's not water, that's jus' cheap vodka, it's just so terrible I haven't drunk it. Yet."

"Where's the bathroom?"

He pointed weakly across the basement. She took the glass with her, dumped it in the sink, and refilled it with water before forcing the cup into his hand.

"Drink it."

"Yes, ma'am."

She shook her head. "Nick, don't you think we belong together?"

"No," he said, shaking his head emphatically. "No, you deserve someone much better than me."

"Don't *I* get to decide that?" Her voice could cut glass now.

"Well, of course, but…"

"Then why would you listen to Cass and stop texting me?"

His eyes widened, a bit of the drunkenness vanishing. "You— you talked to her?"

"Yes. I can't believe her. Or you."

He hung his head. "See. You deserve better."

"I will be the judge of that."

"Don't you wonder at all if she's right? She's your sister."

"So what? That makes her an expert in what I need? Let me tell you, she's rolling a one at this point. This is a complete failure."

"No, Penny. She's right. You deserve someone who can provide

131

for you. Somebody rich. A neurosurgeon. James Bond. I don't know." Maybe he wasn't sobering up after all.

"Most of James Bond's girlfriends end up dead, you do realize."

"Okay, not him. But definitely someone rich."

"Like Cass's husband? Who never comes home?"

"Working hard, I'm sure."

"She thinks he's cheating on her. Gave me a lecture on how men are so fickle."

His mouth fell open. Hadn't expected her to say that.

"Look, I bothered to get this stupid accounting degree. I can provide for myself. I can provide for us both, in fact, while we get our dreams off the ground. My mom and my sister don't know what will make me happy. They don't even know what makes *them* happy. They put all the emphasis on money. And yes, it's important. But they're also miserable."

Her voice softened as she spoke, and she sank beside him on the bed. His eyes followed hers like he was lost at sea and she was the only star in the sky.

"You taught me there are more important things than just money. And I guess I always knew that, but I just didn't have the courage to stand up for it."

She lifted a hand and ran a finger over his jaw, soft as satin. Then she leaned forward and covered his lips with hers.

Of their own accord, his hands reached for her.

Her lips parted beneath his, and he dove into her. She was cool water in a desert, and he a madman, lost and parched and desperate.

Her hands touched his shoulders, pushing him back onto the bed, and he collapsed down. The shadow of her soft, round curves rose up over him, her knees on either side of him, straddling him, powerful.

Something clicked, followed by the feeling of cold metal against one wrist.

"Penny? What the—"

She raised his entrapped wrist above his head, then his free wrist. He didn't resist her, to his own surprise. She circled the cold metal around the wood of the bed frame and clicked it tight around his free hand.

A thrill shot through him.

"Penny, whoa, whoa, slow down," he whispered. He gasped as her lips tickled his throat. "My mom's——"

"Upstairs with *White You Were Sleeping*, a bucket of KFC, and Ashley."

He jerked once against the restraint now. "Ashley?"

"Yeah." Her hot breath danced across his collar as her lips reached the neck of his shirt. "What do you know, turns out she's a good friend after all."

Her hands reached under his shirt, sending shivers through him as her nails dragged against his stomach, up to his chest. Her lips danced across him, leaving a trail of lightning behind them as she made her way up to his ear. He let out a ragged breath.

Her lips brushed his ear lobe. He gasped as her teeth nibbled it, her tongue darting out in a quick swirl.

"I think you may have been a bad boy, Nick Markov," she whispered.

A spark of desire flew through him, and he arched under her, hungry to feel his body against hers. And not just because of her breath tickling his ear.

"I thought I was doing what you would have wanted. Respecting your family's wishes."

She bit his ear again, harder this time, and he sucked in a sharp breath.

"You thought I would give you up just because they told me to?" Penny's face rose over him.

"She seemed to have some valid points that you'd be better off without me."

"She seems full of shit, if you ask me. And since I'm the one who handcuffed you to the bed..." She smiled and raised her eyebrows. "Guess that makes me right."

"You gave up your art. I thought for sure I didn't——"

She crushed his mouth with hers, cutting off the words, her tongue diving even as her fingers went for his belt. Except with pajamas, no belt was necessary. "Mmm," she purred. "Easy access."

"Wait—" He tried to reach for her, but the cuffs caught against the bed frame.

She stopped, bringing her face over his again, eyes boring into his darkness. "I want *you*, Nick. And only you. Not James Bond."

Something in him quivered at those words, words he'd never expected to hear again. But he hadn't stopped her, so she could profess her undying love to him. "Pen, I'm really sorry. I should have talked to you about what Cass said first."

She smiled, then shook her head, sudden mischief twinkling in her eyes. "Told you you've been a bad boy. But apology accepted." Her hand reached for his waistband again, then tickled the trail of hair that led below.

"Wait—wait—tell me. How'd my handcuffs get to your place?"

"Those are my handcuffs. I bought them, got them out so we could use them."

His eyes widened. "You bought handcuffs? That's so sweet. And so, *so* hot."

"Thank you." She grinned. "Now can we continue?"

He glanced up at the cuffs, then back at her uneasily. "You sure about this?"

"Did you know there are people that like both, Nick?"

"Both what?"

"Both top and bottom. Switches. Want to find out if you're one?"

"Okay," he whispered.

But even as her lips brushed his neck again, he already knew the answer.

He shuddered as her hand drifted lower, and she closed her hand around his length. His hips rebelled, pushing toward her, pumping, aching for her.

"Down, tiger," she whispered.

He eased himself back to the bed as she tightened her grip, then let her fingers wander across his stomach, swirl the trail of hair that led south. His skin was alive, electric under her hands. The biting, cold metal against his wrists was reassurance, was power, was surrender...

Was everything.

"Are you sure——" His eyes flicked toward the stairs.

"Yes, I'm very sure. Now shut up."

Her teeth nipped at his neck, then his shoulder, delicate twists of pain. Then she stood and shucked off her pants. He caught a glimpse of smiling strawberries on her underwear before they vanished into the darkness. She bent down eased his pajamas and boxers down over his hips, waiting for his help. His cock, when it finally escaped its flannel prison, bounced up as if to say, *Hello there!* He snorted.

Smiling, she knelt on the bed, gathering his blankets for cover, shifting till she straddled him. Warmth radiated from her as she lowered herself. Slick warmth brushed his cock. So ready, so soon... She'd missed him.

"Penny, what if they come down. There's no hiding this. I——"

"Shh." She closed her fingers over his mouth, and he inhaled sharply at the blast of arousal that shot through him. "In fact, I think you're overthinking this." She leaned toward the end of his bed and grabbed her discarded scarf as he panted for breath.

Then suddenly she was tying it over his eyes. Touch and smell and taste took over the world. A shiver ripped through him, electric with need for her. He tensed and squirmed, trying to reach her skin against his. She waited, silent and unmoving until he stilled. He imagined she was smiling.

"Now, would you say I'm capable of making my own choices?"

"Of course."

She rewarded hum with a kiss, her tongue sweet and minty and aggressive against his. "Good ones, even?"

"You know I do."

A foil wrapper ripped open, and he unintentionally jerked against the handcuffs. He flexed against the bed frame as her deft fingers rolled the condom on.

Please, God, let his mother stay uncurious and selfish with the fried chicken for at least fifteen more minutes. He *really* needed his own apartment.

His stomach twisted with nerves, the air cool on his skin. He was dying to reach for her, aching.

"Then don't forget this is my decision," she whispered, breath tickling his neck.

He nodded, the gesture feeling woefully inadequate. Her fingers caressed his cheek, combed through his beard a few times, and then curled over his mouth again. At the same time, she lowered herself over him.

He gasped for air against her fingers. The world was reduced to her and only her. Her cinnamon roll scent, her molten body overtaking his, the tightness clenching his wrists, his mouth, his cock. And she moved so deliciously, slow like honey, her mouth peppering his shoulders and chest with soft nips.

He might just die. It was too intense. He couldn't take it.

Her fingers dug into the back of his neck, then his right shoulder as she rode him, picking up speed. The soft peaks of her nipples brushed his chest. He could barely keep up, barely survive. She might disagree, but he was definitely sure he didn't deserve his mind blown this thoroughly, not after what he'd done.

My decision... Her words floated back. Right.

Senses half starved for her, he didn't know how it happened or what her other hand was doing, but he managed to sustain himself until he heard a soft velvet gasp. He knew that gasp all too well.

Her core quaked around him, her arm slung around his neck now for balance. Perfection. He arched into her, the bed frame convulsing in time with his thrusts.

Blood slowing, she dropped her forehead to his shoulder, her hair whispering across his chest. There was something precious in that moment, something that he wanted to pull close and hold onto forever.

They panted against each other, sweat slicked across their skin, until he felt her shoulders start to shake.

"Penny? What is it?" He frowned, still trying to catch his breath.

"I was the one to chain Markov to the bed, not the other way around." She giggled softly and pulled the scarf down off his eyes. Her skin was flushed and glowing, eyes bright. How had he thought he could live without her?

He blinked at her, smiling in the darkness. "I have no idea what you're talking about."

"Math joke. I'll explain later."

NICK WAS STILL NOT COMPLETELY SOBER when he piled into Ashley's car with Pen. He was getting there, though. Which was good, because otherwise he would have thought this entire situation was a dream.

Ash dropped them off at Penny's, and he followed her upstairs in a daze. A relieved, relaxed, grateful daze that he wasn't sure he wanted to wake up from.

"We're home," she said as she stopped in front of her door.

We're home. Those were good words, spoken without any hesitation. He followed her inside.

She shut the door and locked it. "So, what should we do now? Make something to eat, watch a movie, go back to bed..." Her eyes twinkled.

"Are you kidding me? Once was definitely not enough." He grabbed her hand and pulled her toward her bed. *While You Were Sleeping* had barely lasted two hours. They had some catching up for lost time to do. And new sexual modes to explore.

Later, as she drifted in and out of sleep, he lay there—awake and sober now and marveling. How could this really have worked out?

As the evening faded, she finally stirred, propping herself up on an elbow under the sheets beside him. "Whatcha thinking about?"

"We had some things we needed to talk about. Before even all this happened."

A soft smile lit her face. "Handcuff sorts of things?"

"Yes. And what you talked about with Ashley."

She threw a hand over her face. "Gosh, that seems so long ago now."

"I'd rather leave Ash in the past. But I do wonder what you talked about."

"She was pretty determined to tell me about your past sex life. And hers. I mostly cut her off. But maybe you should tell me so she doesn't get the chance to spoil the surprise. Although I have my guesses at this point."

He raised his eyebrows at the twinkle in her eyes. "Okay, that's a fair point. Well, let's see. Ash was, uh, creative in bed. I had a point where I was very, very ready to give up my virginity, and—"

"I know the feeling." She smiled.

"You do? Anyway, she was way, *way* over my head. It seemed only open-minded of me to try what she wanted me to. Trying new things, that's what college is about, right?" He fidgeted with the sheet that covered her, then inched a little closer. "I figured maybe after a while I'd like it."

"You didn't like 'it' at first?"

"Some, yes. Some, no. She can be very… domineering."

"She mentioned that."

"Did she. Well, she had her domineering moods. But not always. Things started to get really… complicated."

"Complicated how?"

"Well, I had my domineering moments too."

"I'll bet!"

He stifled a laugh.

"But she could never let go. She had to be in control of those too." The truth was that ultimately Ash was always the one in control. She could be tied up, and she'd still be the catalyst, barking orders. There had been days early on when he'd thought he'd liked it, but for some reason, those feelings had stopped. "She'd still be giving orders, even if on the surface it might have seemed like I was in control. And that was… not for me, I guess? But I couldn't get her to stop it. She didn't care."

Penny frowned and leaned closer, brushing a kiss across his lips. He captured her and kissed her back, hard, grabbing her face with both hands. Why was he kissing her like this now, like she was oxygen and he was suffocating?

No, she couldn't really know what she was getting into, could she? Handcuffs were toys. She should be running away from him and his twisted inclinations. Before he accidentally got drunk again, tied her to her coffee table, and fucked her silly.

Damn, that did sound good, though.

He pulled away and let his forehead rest against hers. Her silver-blue eyes were like a river in the moonlight.

"She should've listened to you," Penny said.

"It doesn't matter."

"Yes, it does. We'll always listen to each other. You don't need to be afraid."

He frowned. "But I *am* afraid." He hesitated. "The night of Anka's party… I'm sorry about all that."

"Why are you sorry?"

"We should have at least talked about what we did first. We were both drunk, and—"

"I really wasn't drunk, Nick." She ran a hand down the side of his face. "I knew what we were doing. I loved every minute of it."

"I'm not even sure I know exactly what happened."

"Oh, well then, let me remind you." To Nick's wide eyes, Penny rattled off an enthusiastic retelling of the evening's misadventures.

"Holy shit, I'm sorry, Penny," he blurted the instant she had finished.

"Why are you sorry? It was basically the hottest thing ever."

"Getting drunk was stupid of me."

"I don't know, we seem to have good luck with it. Don't dodge the question—why are you sorry?"

"I wanted to protect you from the fucked-up. I didn't mean to… get like that with you. Ever."

"Why? We both loved it."

He just stared at her now. "I don't want you to ever do anything you don't want to do."

"I won't. We'll listen to each other, like I said. You don't need to be afraid."

"I feel like I learned all this shit from Ashley, and I can't shake it, and I'm just poisoned forever. And I wanted to protect you from that. From that side of me." He hesitated. "I love you, Penny. I wanted better for you. That's why I listened to Cass."

"Aw, Nick." She leaned closer, and he pressed his forehead against hers. "I love you too. And I love that you want to protect me. But you have to understand that these days, damsels come armed. And you wouldn't want me in your party if I were a level one adventurer with no gear. Would you?"

He chuckled. "I want you in my party no matter what. But we'd get you some gear pronto."

"Well, exactly. And this is *my* adventure, too, Nick. I have a right to explore the parts of it I want to. Just like you have."

"I'm not sure I really wanted to explore all of those... regions."

"That's the real problem. And we won't repeat those mistakes. Okay?"

"But how do we—"

"Safe words."

"What?" His eyes snapped fully open now.

"And limits we talk about ahead of time."

"You... seem to know a lot about this."

"God, I have the internet, Nick. And romance novels. And seriously, have you ever even *watched* anime?"

"No..."

"Do you realize that tentacle-rape porn is a whole sub-genre?"

"What!"

"It's not my thing, I'm just saying, I'm not a kid. I'm a woman. Let's forget about all that stuff in the past. And the guilt. Did you like the handcuffs or not?

"Well... yes."

"Then, let's go on this encounter together and figure out what we like together. Independent of the bullshit."

He pulled her tighter against him. "Figure it out on our own?"

"Yes."

"That... might work. But I mean, but do you really like me..." He stopped, at a loss for words.

"Holding me down and having your way with me?"

He winced. "Yeah."

"Smacking my ass?"

He winced harder. "Fuck. Yes, that too."

"Don't forget collaring me like a dog and making me beg for it."

"Pen, don't tease, I—"

"I like it all very, *very* much, in fact. Want to do it again right now? Want me to meow?"

He burst out laughing. He did, in fact, want to do it again right now. As she'd probably noticed, discussion of those particular activities had gotten him hard again and jabbing impatiently at her hip.

"Think of it like this. It's just more role-playing, right?"

He blinked. "What?"

"Is there so much difference?" She shrugged. "Kids playing cops and robbers don't actually want to *be* cops and robbers. You're bossy with orcs, why not bossy with me in bed?"

Holy shit. He had never made the connection. They were two separate and distinct parts of his life.

Or maybe they weren't. He stared at her, speechless.

"It has not escaped my notice that you prefer to control the games, Nick."

"Nah, it's not like that, I'm just facilitating their fun."

She narrowed her eyes at him. "I look forward to you facilitating my 'fun' later, dungeon master. I think it's more the same than you think. It's just another game."

"A really bad game." He shook his head. "Isn't it disrespectful? I want it, okay, I'll admit it, but *why* do I want it?"

She shrugged one shoulder. "Did you feel disrespected when I took control?"

"Hell no." He felt... important, almost worshipped.

"I felt like I could lose myself. Like I could finally relax. I could admit how damn much I wanted you when you told me to, but not before. I'm supposed to be this good little girl. And I can throw off those expectations and be someone else. Just go crazy with what you do to me. It's exciting. But also safe. I know I'm safe with you."

He gathered her close and squeezed her against him. "Have I told you how amazing you are?"

"Yes."

"Well, you're even more amazing than I knew."

"No."

"Yes. You are." She opened her mouth as if to disagree again. He pressed a finger to her lips, eyes twinkling. "No arguing that, Penny."

"Oooh, hello again, Mr. Markov." She gave his finger a nibble. "What can I do for you today? You're starting to use that voice on me, so whatever you say, as long as you—"

His fingers still against her soft cheek, he leaned forward and pressed a firm kiss against her lips, quieting her. Then he took a deep breath, both to steady himself and to take her in.

He searched her face. How was it possible? What would Ashley think if she knew that her "puppies and rainbows" friend actually wanted him to hold her down and fuck her senseless? And who knew what else. The idea and the image it evoked kicked his craving into high gear—just as Penny opened her mouth and sucked his finger inside. He groaned, hazy images of thrusting his dick into her mouth resurfacing. He snatched his finger back. If she wanted him in charge, he'd give it to her, but this was not that. "You are a kinky woman, Ms. Collins."

"I'd never deny it. Can we please have sex again?" She grinned wickedly at him and lowered her voice, husky and timid now. "Please?"

The bare whisper drove him wild with desire. "When I say so, and not before. Which just coincidentally happens to be right fucking now."

As he pushed her back and rose up over her, he let his tongue play across her skin, remembering her every curve, cherishing every soft gasp.

Who would have thought? He *had* had a chance. Penny wanted him, family and all else be damned.

She wanted him, darkness and all. She had her own darkness, and she wasn't afraid. And yet, with her, it hadn't seemed so dark.

With her, the moon was rising.

Epilogue

PENNY HAD JUST DOZED off for the second time during her CPA practice exam when her phone vibrated.

"What is it, Mom? This isn't a good time." She yawned into the receiver.

"Everything okay, honey?"

"Yep, everything's fine. What is it?"

"Oh, I just wanted you to thank your boyfriend for sending over those pictures. Andrew was delighted. He hadn't thought to commemorate the event. He even ordered pizza for the office tomorrow. Not that I'm going to eat it, but…"

Penny blinked the sleep from her eyes. Was she dreaming? "Oh, I'm sure you could treat yourself to just one piece."

"You haven't seen all the junk I've been eating. And I barely leave my desk. But anyway, I just wanted to say I'm so happy you found a nice boy you're happy with. I'm just so happy to see you happy."

"Wow. Thanks, Mom."

"Why do you sound so surprised?"

"Guess I just wasn't expecting that."

"Everything all right?"

"Yes, yes. It is now, Mom. Thanks for calling. I'll tell Nick you liked them."

"And tell him Andrew liked them. They're special to him. You know, practical arts like ours are important, but Andy will take pride in that photo for a long, long time."

She smiled. "I'll tell him. Good night, Mama."

"Good night, dear."

Nick wandered in, setting down his camera bag at his new desk across from hers. "Who was that?"

"My mom. Wanted to let you know her boss Andrew loved those pictures of their anniversary party."

"Oh. Cool."

He didn't know the rarity of that praise; he'd probably heard the value of photos a million times. She eyed him as he put his things away, relishing the way his tall form moved through her apartment. *Their* apartment now. "Did Regina get back to you yet?"

"Yeah, she wants three more covers. We might do a whole twenty or thirty photos this time. She loved the last two. You up for painting them?"

"Would I let you down, darling?"

"Are you just trying to get out of studying for the exam?"

"Maybe." She grinned.

"Well, because I'm sure you'll do fine and you've probably already studied enough anyway, I'll say no, you'd never let me down." He strode over and kissed the top of her head. "But Regina's got two friends beating down my door for their own shoots. So you better get busy."

"Yes, sir, Mr. Markov." And she turned back to her computer with a wink.

Afterword

Hope you enjoyed *Bad Game*. I'd love if you'd leave a review at your favorite retailer.

If you haven't already, check out the first book in the series, *Good Game*. It's got PC gaming, physics doctorates, and a pretend relationship—fun!

For news on upcoming *Leveling Up in Love* romances, including Ashley's and Olivia's stories, sign up for my newsletter at www.katalexcrystal.com!

And you'll also get Penny's recipe for dark chocolate raspberry brownies.

Happy reading!

25431108R00090

Printed in Great Britain
by Amazon